LIGHT AND DARK

and Other Stories

by Walter Lockwood

Chapbook Press

Schuler Books
2660 28th Street SE
Grand Rapids, MI 49512
(616) 942-7330
www.schulerbooks.com

Light and Dark and Other Stories

ISBN 13: 9781966196297

Library of Congress Control Number: 2025915825

Copyright © 2025 Walter Lockwood

Cover Art and Design by Alexandre Aubertin

All rights reserved. No part of this book may be reproduced in any form except for the purpose of brief reviews or citations without the written permission of the author.

Characters, names, places and incidents are the products of the author's imagination and are used fictitiously.

Printed in the United States by Chapbook Press.

To Dr. Clinton Burhans, mentor and master
teacher.

Special thanks to those who read or listened and offered insights
and encouragement: my wife Pam, daughters Katie, Susan, Alison,
and son Matt; my sister Susie, sister-in-law Kim, and friends G.F.
Korreck, Jeffrey Petersen, Eli Petersen, Dave Hendrickson, and
David Wygmans.

In a dark time, the eye begins to see.

—*Theodore Roethke*

CONTENTS

OCTOGENARIAN

It was early morning, first light, and Henry Brandt sat in bed reading *The Atlantic*—an article maintaining that most older people felt 20% younger than they actually were. He was eighty but for him 40% felt more accurate. There was a young thing in him that stayed that way because he wrote. Stories often came to him without any time between—a steady stream. He'd written many in the last four years and published two collections. Lately, though, they were arriving more slowly. His latest idea refused to grow. He had noticeably less energy, and he felt hazy and light-headed. He couldn't focus. The life he now lived was part of the problem. His solitude of the last ten years, since his wife's death, had been gone for several months, but he'd had little choice in the matter. His daughter Helen was struggling, and her daughter Beatrice, known as Birdie, was now his responsibility during the day while Helen worked.

One of the cats—Oscar, the black male—lay stretched out flat on his lap. Harriet, the grey female, slid through the door with a squawk. "Get going," she was saying to him. Her right ear was split where a raccoon had clawed it. Oscar leapt off the bed. Henry set aside the magazine and maneuvered to his feet, hoping to go directly into the shower but hearing Helen already in there.

So he shuffled downstairs in his slippers and pajamas to feed the cats. He put away pots and pans from the night before and emptied the dishwasher with the usual clatter, knowing nothing would wake Birdie. He ground coffee and made it the way Helen liked it—strong with a touch of hazelnut. It was April, and the morning sun showed up the winter's film of fingerprints and smudges on the windows. He went outside into the back garden to fill the bird feeders. The squirrels were so accustomed to him they didn't dive off the feeding tubes until he reached for the caps. Both cats hung near his feet, chattering at birds in the nearby cedars. They were too old and slow to be a threat. The birds knew it, and as soon as Henry had poured in the black oilers, they returned to the feeders, chickadees first. The cats sat watching, a daily pantomime of predator and prey.

The back yard was devoted mainly to his large vegetable garden, which he would plant in a few weeks even though it was getting too much for him. He hoped Birdie might help him, but her limitations were many. She and her mother had lived with him four months now, and he had no clear sense yet of what Birdie could do. She was eighteen but still a child in most ways.

His house was the oldest in the neighborhood, a white frame farmhouse built before land around it had been sold for development. He kept the place fairly presentable, though it needed paint again and probably a roof. He'd managed all of that himself once, but now he had to hire it done. Helen helped on the inside, but the rest was up to him. Some days he wished he were truly as young as he felt when he wrote.

With the birds seen to, he returned to the kitchen, poured a cup of coffee, and sat down at the counter. Helen rushed into the room, dumped coffee into his favorite travel mug. She was, as always, running late and didn't have time to sit.

"Birdie's lunch is wrapped in foil in the fridge," she said brusquely. "No Coke for her today…try to get some milk into her. The sugar is ruining her teeth, as if she didn't have enough complications." She bent to pull on her white tennis shoes without untying them. "Please do something constructive with her today, Dad. Don't let her just sit and stare at television."

He was working hard every day at being calm about her negativity, especially concerning things he wasn't guilty of. "I'll be taking her to the store. She'll be out helping get the garden ready, too. Tons to do out there."

"Good luck with that," she said with a short, ironic laugh. "I'm not sure what you're expecting."

He looked at his daughter, at the angular body, the spiky red hair, the tattooed arms, the sharp-edged, aging face—a stranger who, at thirty-nine, had appeared out of some other life, needing him suddenly after twenty years.

She handed him a list of things she wanted from the store. Though she'd found work as a receptionist in an orthodontist's office, she hadn't yet begun giving him money for expenses. He knew she was paying off debts for Birdie's health care and therapy, for special schools, and for her own careless living. From her late teens until now, Helen had rarely communicated with her parents. They'd only seen Birdie twice—as an infant and then at six or so. At her mother's death, Helen had sent a letter explaining she was in a west coast hospital and couldn't make the funeral. Her older brother had flown in from England where he taught in a university.

Henry had learned from an assortment of her former friends that Helen, after dropping out of college at nineteen, traveling the country as backup singer for a punk band, had discovered the performance-enhancing qualities of alcohol and drugs. It was during those years she got pregnant with Birdie. Helen was now a recovering addict, sober at last for good, she told him—but that hadn't fixed whatever was wrong with Birdie. She didn't know who Birdie's father was.

Henry ached for the support of his wife, but her wise presence was gone forever. Helen was an edgy, often angry person, and living with her wasn't easy. But there hadn't been a way to avoid taking her in. She was out of options.

He'd casually connected with several women since his wife's death—more their doing than his. One, a former English Department colleague, a widow, had begun to get serious about him, but her four kids and multiple grandkids were a daily part of her life. He'd enjoyed her company, but all the extras required so much time and effort that he'd slowly, carefully backed away. Considering his present situation, it was a good thing he had.

He watched Helen roll her ancient Grand Prix out of the driveway and roar off down the street. The muffler system was rusting out—dual pipes, mufflers, and resonators, a small fortune to replace. The shocks were gone, but, as with her life, she ignored the instability and kept rolling.

Henry took a quick shower, dressed in worn khakis and a flannel shirt, ate a bowl of oatmeal with brown sugar and fruit, and went into his upstairs office, his wife's former sewing room, excited to resume work. He still made preliminary notes in longhand on legal sheets, but his composing these days was done on his computer. Birdie slept like the dead twelve or more hours a night, giving him several uninterrupted morning hours to write. How did she manage such sleep? His own was shallow, sporadic, troubled. He got much of his reading done in the middle of the night.

The middle-aged spinster church organist he had hopes for as a character rode her stationary bike daily as she prayed through her rosary in a dull, mechanical mumble. Her two cats, curled in chairs, seemed hypnotized by the drone. From her spot in the den, she had a clear view through a slim beveled window of people ringing the doorbell—assertive-looking women with petitions, dark-suited Jehovah's Witnesses, boys seeking donations for their teams, timid adolescents selling Girl Scout cookies. She rarely answered the bell. She could see all solicitors, but they couldn't see her.

Henry liked strangers walking into his stories, so he'd imagined an unusual solicitor…and on a day threatening rain. This one was a thin, bearded man who looked somewhere near forty. He leaned heavily on her doorbell, then knocked and would not stop. At last, she jumped angrily from her bike, went to the door, and threw it open. She cast him her severest glare, yet he stood calm and unruffled. His arched eyebrows and slightly slanted eyes seemed wolf-like. It took a moment for her to notice he was missing a hand, his left. He waited without a word until she asked, "Is there something you want?"

"You have a problem with your house," he said. He told her he was a carpenter and needed to show her just what he meant. She wondered how a one-handed carpenter managed his work.

Without really understanding why, besides the start of rain, she invited him inside. He said he was working in the neighborhood and noticed the problem walking by. He went to the nearer of the two front windows, raised it, removed a screwdriver from his carpenter's belt, and pushed it into the sill. It went in like a knife into a melon. She was shocked. "Rot," he said. "These sills are like pulp. So are the lower frames. There's water getting in. It'll need seeing to. Window replacement would be best."

He looked into the den and noticed her rosary hanging on the handlebar of her stationary bike. "Beautiful rosary. Looks like black onyx. My wife had one like it. I've kept it."

"Have you? And do you use it?"

He shook his head. "I've fallen away from the faith since she passed."

Henry stopped and stared at the computer screen. Why was he a one-handed carpenter? What was that about? His reading had a way of leaking into his work at times. Was it Flannery O'Connor?

He was startled suddenly by Birdie banging around in the bathroom. Something clattered to the floor—the metal soap dish, he guessed, or a hairbrush. Birdie was small and clumsy as a bear cub. He glanced at his watch and was shocked to see it was 12:35. Where had the morning gone? He'd moved the story just inches.

He rose from his battered office chair and found Birdie in misbuttoned pink pajamas standing in the doorway.   A miniature person, not quite five feet tall, she had a tiny head with a helmet of white blonde hair cut by her mother, wide-set eyes, and the flat face of a Persian cat—an unusual presence that took some getting used to. Her body was boyish except for moderately developed breasts that he sometimes saw her touching as if newly discovering them. Her eyes rarely met his.

"Are you writing a story, Papa?"

"Yes, Birdie."

"Did I read yesterday? I don't remember."

She could read—at perhaps a second-grade level, afflicted as she was with a puzzling assortment of learning disabilities. Her memory was the thinnest of threads, but he'd found a way into her mind: she loved listening to simple stories for young people—Helen's books from childhood. By "her reading" she meant his reading to her. It was enjoyable for him, and while he did it, Birdie's exaggerated facial expressions resembled silent movie acting. "Nancy Drew, *The Hidden Staircase*. Remember?"

"I think so."

"We'll read more today. Get dressed and I'll put out something to eat."

Except for sweets and salty snacks, Birdie was the pickiest of eaters. She nibbled at the edges of the peanut butter sandwich her mother had left, her mouth open as she chewed. Henry brought out some sliced ham from the night before and a spoonful of deli potato salad for himself. He offered her small raw carrots, but she ignored them. She hated most vegetables, would eat only certain fruits if they were prepared correctly. Apples had to be peeled and sliced. Grapes were to be green, seedless, and detached from spidery vines. She was awkward with utensils and preferred her fingers, and at home even Helen tended to acquiesce to that.

At the grocery store later, Birdie walked ahead of the cart, finding things she wanted and bringing them to him. They were always snacks, and he asked her in a gentle, patient way to put them back. It was an odd little game, a part of the grocery store experience. Just once—some weeks ago—he'd snapped impatiently at her for doing it too many times, and she'd run away in tears, hiding herself among boxes in a rear storage room. It'd taken security a half hour to find her.

She went ahead of him now in breakfast cereals as he searched for Quaker Oats. When he glanced up a moment later, she'd disappeared around the end of the aisle. He hurried to make the turn himself, but she was nowhere in sight. For just an instant, he felt panic. He raced down the side aisle, looking the length of each center aisle as he passed. His heart resumed beating when he spotted her in the candy section, holding a giant package of chocolate eggs on sale from Easter.

"One half off," she said, smiling broadly as he caught up to her.

"Yes, Birdie, great price," he said through heavy breathing. A familiar light-headedness made him unsteady on his feet. "But your mom would be mad at us."

Her face reddened, but to his great relief she calmed herself and put the package back. "She's mean."

"She's trying to keep us healthy, honey. Come on, let's finish up and get home. We'll sit on the couch and read Nancy Drew."

He suddenly felt exhausted.

Though she fell asleep once while he was reading to her, for the most part the uninspired story engaged her. Afterwards, they went out into the back garden. He showed her what dandelions looked like, and how to dig them out with a hand trowel. She handled the job slowly but with surprising competence, even getting most of the taproots. He was pleased. Helen would be skeptical of any heightened enthusiasm from him, so he'd learned to understate these small victories. At dinner that night, he mentioned the dandelions in an off-handed manner. As always, Helen seemed doubtful of his report. His family life had become a delicate juggling act. He went to bed that night having given not a thought to his one-handed carpenter.

Because he'd felt moved to do it, Henry employed a yard man named Kenny who lived with his mother somewhere in the neighborhood. Mentally impaired, of indefinite age (Henry guessed mid-thirties), Kenny pushed a blue reel mower around the neighborhood and mowed lawns for a modest price. He came with rakes in spring and fall and shovels in the winter. Henry admired his work ethic even if his results fell short. Henry would smooth the rough edges once Kenny had left.

At the gas station where Kenny hung out, Henry had several times heard him referred to as Bighead. Kenny took no offence—he seemed to like having a nickname. The reason for the name was plain enough: his head was too large for his body—nearly the size of a basketball. He'd somehow found a Tigers cap to fit, and his wiry black hair sprang from it over the tops of his ears. He talked little and had trouble pronouncing certain words. Lawn mower came out "long more." Snow shoveling came out "snow shubbling." He overheated quickly on summer days, and Henry sometimes carried lemonade out to him and made him sit on the porch in the shade until the red in his face paled to light pink.

Kenny showed up at the end of the week for the first spring mowing. The yard was ragged and full of sticks, leaves, and other winter litter, so Kenny raked up most of it before he mowed. Birdie, who had just eaten lunch, went out on the porch to watch him. Henry sat with her, sipping coffee as she drank from a juice box. When Kenny finished mowing, he came over and stood on the steps.

"Kenny, I want you to meet my granddaughter Birdie," Henry said. "She and her mother are living with me now."

"Hi," Birdie said, looking at her lap.

Kenny nodded, glancing quickly at her and then away.

"What do I owe you today?"

"Ten bucks."

Henry gave him fifteen. Kenny stared at it a moment, then stuffed it in his jeans. "The extra is for raking. You earned it."

"I dug up dandelions in the garden," Birdie told him, not looking up.

Kenny seemed surprised. "I do that sometimes, too," he said. He abruptly stood to go. "I got more long moring. G'bye."

"Have a good day," Henry said.

"Have a good day," Birdie repeated.

The one-handed carpenter, Henry decided, had been that way from birth. His stump was almost as efficient as a hand. He had fashioned a prosthetic device to hold a nail in place while he hammered. The spinster church organist hired him to replace the two front windows, which he did for what seemed a reasonable price. She had him check windows throughout the house, and he replaced three more. In return for her business, he brought along his wife's rosary, and they sometimes prayed through the decades aloud, taking turns. This exercise was very satisfying to her, and she looked forward to his being there. She found more for him to do. After three weeks, he began entering the house early mornings without knocking. It felt almost as if she had a husband. The more he worked, the more he appeared to take ownership in the house. It had to do with pride in his work. She deduced from his aging pickup truck that he certainly wasn't well-to-do—no doubt because he was more concerned with craftsmanship than with making money. She was like that, too. In important ways, they were much the same.

Henry's story, of course, was not heading toward love and happiness. God forbid. But Henry hadn't decided whether the one-handed carpenter was hustling the spinster church organist or vice versa. He needed more time to think, but his days were too full of other agendas. Still, the story was straining to assume a shape.

On the first of May, Kenny returned with his lawn mower. To Henry's surprise, Birdie took a seat on the porch and quietly watched the process. Kenny waved once to her before he left. The next week, when he'd finished mowing, he climbed the porch steps and sat down in the wicker chair next to her. He said "Hi, Birdie." Henry stood at an open window watching. Birdie didn't look at Kenny but seemed to be smiling faintly. They sat silently for half an hour before Kenny left.

To his relief, Birdie was actually a help getting the garden in. She liked planting seeds, especially the beets—big enough for her awkward hands to manage. She carefully placed the seeds half an inch deep and an inch apart, far more precisely than Henry ever had (though she took forever doing it). Once she dug up a large stag beetle, wailed like a fire siren, and then hid in the utility shed until Henry had squashed the beetle and calmed her down with a chocolate bar.

Kenny kept coming and Birdie kept waiting on the porch. Henry moved his legal pads and computer to the dining room table so he could watch and work. He imagined something unexpected, perhaps even grisly for his story's climax, but he didn't yet know what it was.

Birdie and Kenny spoke a bit more often. He told her about buying his lawn mower from a garage sale for eight bucks. She told him she had two cats. Sometimes he stayed for more than an hour after he mowed. Once, with Henry along, she took Kenny out to the garden and showed him the beet sprouts pushing through the ground, a miracle to her. Kenny knelt down to look and seemed impressed. In some mostly silent way, they'd made a connection. Birdie didn't mention him to Helen; it appeared to be her secret. Henry thought it wise to follow her lead. He appreciated the time Kenny bought him, even though the story mulishly refused to be pushed.

In spite of his limitations, Kenny seemed to Henry a gentle, hard-working person. Birdie was quiet and calm with him. Henry suspected she needed a friend as much as Kenny did. Following his Friday visits, Birdie ate more than usual. She raised no fuss about television programs or bedtime.

"She's a bit like me—better natured on Fridays," Helen said once, but Henry made no comment.

One Saturday morning while Birdie was still in bed, Henry sat having coffee with Helen in the kitchen, talking about Birdie getting a job. If patiently trained, Henry maintained, she could do repetitive work very well. He'd seen it in the garden. Helen was listening but skeptical. She couldn't imagine Birdie, as unpredictable as she was, venturing into the world.

They heard a light knock at the front door, and Helen got up to answer. Henry followed her. She opened to Kenny standing at the door in his Tigers cap.

"Yes?" Helen said impatiently.

"Can Birdie sit with me on the porch?"

Helen stiffened. "Who are you?"

"I'm Kenny. I'm the long more guy."

"Birdie can't come out. She's asleep."

"Are you her mother?"

"Yes."

His mouth drooped. "Oh." And he turned and left.

Helen swung her eyes to Henry. "Who the hell was *that*?"

"He's my lawn guy."

"Is he retarded?"

"He's mentally disabled."

"He wanted to sit on the porch with Birdie."

"What's the problem? They're friends."

"What possible good is a person like that going to do her?"

"What harm is he going to do her?"

"Honestly, Dad, you can be so naïve."

They returned to the kitchen just as Birdie appeared in pajamas, still half asleep.

"Who was here?" she asked her mother.

"Nobody important."

"Who was it?"

"Some guy."

"Was it Kenny?"

Helen glanced at Henry. "That's what he said. Who is he?"

"A boy I know," Birdie answered.

"The one you sit with on the porch?"

"Yes."

"What else do you do?"

"We talk. I like him. Maybe we'll get married some time."

Helen's laugh sounded half crazed. "Oh my god…there's a happy thought."

Henry was dismayed at his daughter. "Helen…for heaven's sake…"

Birdie fortunately couldn't process irony. "Yes, it is." She looked from Helen to Henry and back, and then she turned and went back upstairs.

"Fire your lawn guy," Helen ordered.

"No, Helen. He's been with me for three years. There's no reason. I'm always around. I watch them."

"I know you. You may be here in body, but your mind is off in story land. Get rid of Kenny."

"I won't do it. He's a kind, simple guy, and she's a kid. She's just fantasizing. Birdie needs a life and friends as much as any of us."

"She's not a kid, Dad. She's eighteen." She took a deep breath and exhaled heavily. "Okay, I'm making this your responsibility. "

"Fine," he said. "Just have a little faith."

"In what?" she asked sullenly.

The church organist and the carpenter had dinner and a bottle of sparkling wine at her house in celebration of his fortieth birthday. She was forty-six but hadn't mentioned it to him. It was Sunday, and he'd gone to mass that morning to hear her play a Bach prelude and an Elgar postlude. She'd baked a layer cake and decorated it with "Happy 40th" and four large candles. The wine warmed them; he took her hand and held it.

Though she hoped he might spend the night, he left at ten, disappointing and pleasing her at the same time. He was a gentleman. Her faith and limited experience with men made her anxious about stepping into the physical part of a relationship. Yet if he made a move in that direction, she knew she wouldn't resist. Instead of putting her off, his disfigurement somehow aroused her. She was older than he and, though trim, she had seen her modest beauty fade year by year to a spinsterish plainness. Yet somehow his lack of a hand seemed an equalizer. An independent woman, she owned a house and was fully self-supporting, representing stability that he perhaps lacked. He lived in a small apartment, he told her, but she'd never seen it. His late wife had died there.

The organist had fleeting thoughts of marriage and how it might alter her life. But that was thinking too far ahead.

Henry, feeling the story edging forward, saved what he'd written and looked up at the front porch where Birdie and Kenny were sitting. But their chairs were empty. Shocked, disbelieving, he gathered himself and hurried out, glancing up and down the street. He'd lost track of time. How long had they been gone?

Henry half ran to the back yard but found only an empty garden. Trying to control his panic, he considered where these two might go. He nearly called Helen for help but then thought better of it. He locked the front door and began driving the neighborhood. He stopped at the gas station where Kenny hung out. The owl-eyed girl at the counter looked puzzled when he asked if she'd seen Kenny the lawn guy.

"You know…he hangs out here. Wears a Tigers hat. Some of you call him Bighead."

A pony-tailed man stocking shelves said, "Yeah, I know Bighead. Haven't seen him today."

"Do you know where he lives?"

"Over by the Lutheran Church on Elmwood. I think he's sort of an assistant janitor there. Don't know which house. Is he in trouble?"

Henry shook his head. "Not at all, I need him for a job."

"Couple of streets over. Ask the neighbors. Everybody knows Bighead."

Henry could see the steeple of St. John's Lutheran from the gas station. He drove over and parked in front of the church. There wasn't a neighbor to be seen up and down the street, so he tried the front door of the church. It was open, and he spotted a skinny, brittle-looking woman sitting at a computer behind a glass window marked CHURCH OFFICE.

"May I help you?" she asked with a smile full of shiny false teeth.

"I'm looking for Kenny, the guy who mows lawns around this neighborhood. He does mine. I'm afraid I don't know his last name."

"Oh, that's Kenny Simpson. He lives right next door to the church." She pointed out the window at a small red brick house. Kenny's blue hand mower stood beside the porch. "His mother is home, I think, but Kenny is downstairs cleaning right now. He works for us."

"Oh—thank goodness. Would you mind if I went down a minute to see him? I have a job for him."

"Oh, how nice." She pointed the way to the stairs. "I'd take you down, but I'm having a knee replacement soon."

"I'll find my way." Henry felt dizzy as he descended the stairway to the children's worship area. The walls were hung with primitive drawings of fathers for Father's Day, accompanied by "I love Daddy" misspelled in multiple ways within hearts. The stairs led him into a lower hallway with four doors. Each door had a window, so he went from one to the next. Reaching the farthest down, he caught sight of Kenny sitting on a beanbag chair with Birdie beside him. They were eating windmill cookies. Around them were boxes of cardboard blocks, toys, tables scattered with art supplies. A vacuum cleaner stood idle.

Henry went in. Birdie's tee shirt was rumpled and scattered with crumbs.

"Birdie," he said. "You gave me an awful scare. What are you doing?"

"Hi, Papa. We're having some cookies. Kenny works here, so it's okay."

Henry stared at the two. Kenny's right arm encircled her. He looked happy. "Well, I'm afraid it's time to go home. Your mother will be out of work soon. I'm glad you're safe. I wish you'd told me you were coming here."

"I took care of her," Kenny said.

"I can see you did. Thank you, Kenny. Next time tell me before you take her somewhere."

"Okay."

Birdie went along without an objection. Henry heard Kenny begin his vacuuming. On the main floor he slipped out a side door so the secretary wouldn't see them.

The carpenter was up on the back porch roof with a bucket of tar when the phone rang. The church organist answered. No one spoke for several seconds. Then a raspy female voice (a long-time smoker, she suspected) said, "The handyman working for you isn't who he says he is. I'm looking at him right now from my car. He's fixing your roof."

"Who is this?"

"I won't say my name. But I will tell you he's a relative—the shirttail variety. Maybe eight months ago he escaped from a prison work crew in Illinois. Makes me think of one of those wolves that chews off his foot to get out of a trap." She laughed and coughed a bit. "I guess you know what I'm talking about. Something kind of sexy about that stump arm of his." She went silent as if thinking about it. "He usually says he had a wife who died, but truth is he never had a wife. He uses the story to talk softhearted women out of their money and property, and I'm one of them. Don't believe what he tells you.

He just wants what you have. He'll promise to marry you, if he has to."

"He hasn't asked."

"Well, whatever. Go ahead and turn him in if you want. I won't do it because he's family. I'm just telling you as a favor."

"How do I know it's the truth?"

"I guess you don't. I'm parked half a block west on the other side of the street in a red Chevy if you want to talk in person."

She glanced out and saw the red Chevy down the street. "I can see you, but I guess I don't need to talk. I do thank you for your information."

"Glad to be of help to a fellow chump."

The word made the church organist wince. She hung up quickly and moved to the front window to watch the Chevy move up the street. A fairly pretty woman of thirty or so smiled as she passed. The organist filled with rage—more at the young woman than the carpenter. But the blazing anger was gone in a short time, replaced by her usual calm, rational self. Her quiet life, she mused, was taking very unexpected turns these days. She felt almost like a character in a story.

In the beginning of August, the days grew sultry; the garden dried up and required almost daily watering. The yard was brown, but Kenny kept coming to mow. Tomatoes were ripening by the dozens. Henry boiled up beet greens, though Birdie wouldn't touch them in spite of her part in their inception. She seemed to be sick more than usual; Helen grew impatient and hauled her off to a doctor, one that Henry had gone to for years. Henry was worried. Birdie was underdeveloped in so many ways. Her life expectancy, he had read, was thirty-four. He cared about her, he realized, more than he did his own daughter who would probably live to a disagreeable ninety if she didn't destroy herself first.

When they failed to return home after two and a half hours, he began to be concerned. He was about to call the office, when the phone rang. It was Dr. O'Connor, his internist for thirty some years, nearing retirement now, though Henry still thought of him as a young man.

"Henry, we have a problem here," he said. "Your daughter Helen was so disturbed by my diagnosis that she began screaming and stormed off without Birdie. Birdie is very upset. Could you come and get her?"

Henry was stricken. "What's wrong with Birdie?"

He hesitated. "Well, nothing really. She's pregnant."

"Oh my God." It was all Henry could think of to say. "I'm leaving now."

The last book he'd read her was *The Secret Garden*. She'd loved it. So had he. The disabled character in the story had been healed and made whole, and the transformation had brought tears to his eyes. If only life could manage outcomes as well. Birdie was pregnant. Kenny was certainly the father, the child conceived in a church basement. The prospects of a normal child were…well, he didn't know. Not good, for certain. He could never dream up such calamity as this.

The story sat unfinished. At this point there was too much of everyday life going on. Helen had left the doctor's office, driven her Grand Prix like an insane woman, and stopped at a highway bar outside of town. She'd ordered vodka tonics until they refused to serve her any more. Distraught and drunk, she'd run her car into a tree and somehow only broken her nose and an arm. It appeared to be a suicide attempt. She was spending some time in a mental health facility. Her job was in doubt. Henry was now in full charge of Birdie. In many ways it was easier without Helen around. Kenny's mother, a sweet but slightly dotty woman in her sixties, was hysterical at the news of the pregnancy, but she slowly recovered and did her best to help.

Kenny doted on Birdie. They wanted to get married, but Henry investigated and found a myriad of difficulties with SSI and Medicaid. So Kenny's mother arranged a four-person ceremony at her house, and Henry officiated in the creation of a common law union of sorts, which seemed to satisfy all involved. Henry didn't mention the fact to Helen when he visited.

The newlyweds began staying with Henry for a week, followed by a week with Kenny's mother. Oddly enough, life seemed in some ways easier. He had more solitude but also more worries. By next February, he knew (if all went as expected) there would be an infant in their midst. Helen would probably be home again. He couldn't imagine the mix.

The story had limped its way to a conclusion; Henry wasn't at all sure of his mental acuity at this point. Life was so full of its own catastrophes that he had trouble imagining fictional ones.

The church organist, as it turned out, dealt with the one-handed carpenter directly. She waited until he was back inside the house, scrubbed clean of tar but smelling of turpentine. He went into the kitchen, searching the refrigerator for a beer. She followed him, her arms crossed in front of her.

"You aren't who you say you are," she told him.

He looked at her, then took a beer and opened it. "Oh?"

"I know the trouble you're in, and I know what you want from me."

Uneasy, he thought for a few moments and then asked, "What are you going to do?"

"I don't know yet. We'll see. Do you like it here?"

"Mostly."

"You're a good carpenter, even with only one hand. It's helpful having you around."

"The place needs seeing to."

"It does, so I'll make you a deal. You can move in here and keep your made-up name. We can tell people we're married for the sake of appearances, but we won't be, and you'll have no legal right to anything. You can sleep in my bed if you want. But if you try to take things from me, I'll go to the authorities. I'll fix it so that whatever wrong you might do me, they'll find out and put you back in prison."

He stared at her, not speaking for a long while. "I don't much care for that deal."

"Your choice."

"What if I was to leave now?"

"I wouldn't say anything against you."

He hesitated, took a long swallow of beer, and then turned and went to the gas range. "The igniter on this stove is shorting out. Guess I'll fix it."

And just that easily, they were man and wife. The arrangement lasted two years and three months before he went away—disappeared one day, taking nothing of hers with him. Though she missed him at first, the return of solitude was pleasant. She hadn't loved him, but her house and her spirit had undergone improvement, and she felt no regret. Some nights she even dreamed of the wolfish face and his ardent, handless caresses.

Henry put down this final page and sat unmoving at his desk. He noticed the reflection of his face in the blank computer screen. He saw an old man, an octogenarian, soon to be raising a child of some indefinite sort in a house of damaged people. It was a scenario so ludicrous that he laughed out loud. He had ten years to live, maybe less. One couldn't predict such things. There might be time to write a few more stories if he should ever get beyond the one he was presently living in.

OLIVER WISDOM CONTEMPLATES TIME

Oliver Wisdom's summer dreams centered on a grownup woman—one he didn't know except by sight. She lived one door north of his grandparents' house, and from his bedroom he could see her sitting at breakfast, drinking tea in an old-fashioned white nightgown. Her hair was a burnished gold and shining as if she'd just brushed it a hundred strokes. He'd watched since a few days after his arrival, deposited here while his father and mother travelled in Europe. He watched her from a chair by his bedroom window as he read through music he would be performing once his parents returned. This morning it was Bach's "Air on a G String." As he imagined the music, she seemed somehow to embody it—the slow tempo with haunting counterpoint accompanying her graceful movements from table to stove and back. From a distance she looked extremely pretty—he guessed in her early twenties. He was only twelve but well beyond that in intelligence (or so he was told), especially in music.

Once breakfast was done, he wouldn't see her again until the next morning. He wanted to ask his grandparents who she was but felt awkward about it. In his dreams he was older than twelve, actually older than she. They were living together, perhaps even married, in a tiny summer cottage near a river. He remembered in the hazy background of the dream a stern old man, perhaps her father, who disapproved of them. They had run away to this place.

In every dream they walked along the river together listening to its music. A swing hung by two long ropes from the high limb of an oak tree, and he would push her until her feet touched the leaves. He somehow earned a living for the two of them but didn't know at what. The car they drove was a black coupe, like the one he had seen in fading photos of his grandparents when they were young. The woman and he were passionately in love. Their lovemaking was a pleasure he felt intensely yet hypothetically, without concrete specifics. When he woke from the dreams, he rolled to his feet, heart pounding and body aflame. He went to the window chair and waited anxiously for her appearance at breakfast.

Maude Wisdom, his grandmother, was a religious woman with a strong sense of duty to suffering humanity. His grandfather Jeremy Wisdom, editor of a local newspaper, was a cynic who mistrusted the motives of most people, do-gooders in particular. That included his wife and her church. The two of them slept in separate rooms, and he stayed long hours at the newspaper office while she went about her Christian work. Oliver admired his grandfather, appreciated his bluntness, but had never gotten much time with him. His grandmother's determined piety made him deeply uncomfortable. Part of her Christian work involved visiting the convalescent home next door, just to the south, two or three times a week. She was intent on involving him in it.

Oliver's great grandmother lived there, a frail, toothless crone, far gone in dementia. She'd lived with her son and daughter-in-law for some years after her husband died. The bedroom Oliver slept in had been hers (a musty, old woman smell still lingered) until they'd had to move her to the convalescent home when she began to forget how to do things. One day she'd tried to warm her shawl over the gas stove and set fire to the kitchen.

The Brown Convalescent Home was a large, drab, brick structure, former residential home, family-operated and not particularly sanitary, yet affordable and close by. Maude Wisdom made her husband promise he'd never put her there, though it seemed the logical place to put her mother-in-law.

It was Oliver's misfortune that the Home had an ancient piano in the sitting room where the patients, all of them women, gathered to watch the changing weather and discuss it at length. Television sets were still a new form of distraction, and the Brown Home had not yet invested in one. The piano, a battered upright with yellow, cigarette-burned keys, was tinny and desperately out of tune. He'd played three quarters of an hour for the patients on the second day of his visit. Today, as they walked toward the Home, he objected. She'd made him wear his white Sunday shirt and a tie.

"Grandma, I don't want to go again. Please!" He'd dropped a step behind her as they turned up the walkway to the grim fortress.

"She's your great grandmother, Oliver. She's alone all day long. She just loves having a young person visit, especially you."

"It stinks in there. The piano is terrible."

She stopped and waited a moment for him to catch up. "Think of the joy you bring to these lonely women. We all need to share our gifts." She took his arm and guided him through the front door. The air felt clammy and wet. A tall, angular nurse with straight black hair rose from her seat at a cluttered desk. She was dressed all in white, including her pointy cap.

"Good morning, Mrs. Wisdom," she said, revealing large equine teeth. "She's been waiting for you. Hello, young man. How nice to see you again. Go right in."

Maude Wisdom smiled sweetly. "Yes, thank you, Josephine," she replied in her benign voice and led him toward room seven. She pulled open the door and maneuvered Oliver over to a wheelchair with his great grandmother tucked tightly into it.

The old woman's eyes were small and opaque, the oldest part of her, lost in fold upon fold of sagging skin like raisins in a pudding. Oliver was certain he would never be that old.

"Hello, Mother. Look who I have with me!"

The old woman reached for Oliver's hand, her voice squawking, parrot-like. "Oh, my! Are you my little boy?"

Oliver pulled his hand away, but his grandmother gave him a look. Reluctantly, he allowed the aged woman to grasp his fingers.

"Are you my little Jeremy?"

"This is Oliver, Mother. He's Jeremy's grandson, remember?"

"Oh, of course he is. Am I going home now?"

Maude Wisdom took a deep breath. "Not today, Mother. Maybe soon."

"I want to go home. This is an awful place. It stinks. They aren't nice to me."

"Mrs. Brown and all the nurses seem very nice."

"They're mean. I'm afraid of them." She limply squeezed Oliver's hand. "Want a mint, Jeremy? I have bags and bags of mints. Are you my little boy?"

Oliver pulled his hand away and glanced pleadingly at his grandmother.

"Give Gertic a mint," his great grandmother squawked. Oliver became aware of another woman lying in bed across the room. He'd hardly noticed her in his previous visit.

The woman pulled the sheet up to her nose and turned away. Her voice was thin and emotional. "I don't want a mint. And please stop calling me Gertie. My name is Georgia."

His great grandmother ignored her. "Gertie always gets upset. Jesus visits me every day but not her because she's mean as an old badger." She shoved mints in Oliver's hand and pointed the way to the woman. He took several steps in her direction.

"Jesus never comes here," the woman hissed. "It's too terrible even for him."

"I pray for Gertie every day. She came from the poor house."

"I did not! I don't want you praying for me!"

Almost against his will, something compelled Oliver toward the woman. He stood at her bedside and held out the candy. She pushed his hand away and raised her head to look at him.   A point of light brightened in her eyes for just an instant. *"You,"* she said, as if she knew him.

Puzzled, he nodded and said, "I was here a few days ago."

"It was years ago."

"I'm only twelve."

"Time doesn't matter here." She lowered her head to the pillow.

"Come on and eat your mints, Gertie," his great grandmother wheedled. "They'll sweeten you up."

A small, dog-like moan came out of the woman. "Can't you see what it's like? Can't you take her out and give me a few minutes of peace?"

Oliver stared into her pleading eyes. They were teary and inflamed yet younger by far than his great grandmother's. Something stirred in him, and he began wondering about her in a way he'd never wondered about anyone.

"Oliver is going to play for all of the ladies, Mother," Maude Wisdom said. "We'll wheel you down to the sitting room. He's a lovely pianist, especially for his age."

The woman in the bed turned to the wall.

The sitting room windows were hazy and their frames heavy with a century of paint. A number of old ladies had already arrived when Oliver rolled in his great grandmother and moved her into a line of other wheelchairs. Several ladies in the wheelchairs were knitting as deftly as machines. Another was asleep, her chin tucked impossibly into her neck. Two more, still mobile, played dominoes in folding chairs at a table.

When he'd performed for them two days before, they'd smiled blankly in response to Bach and Mozart. One or two had applauded, but with hands like damp leaves. Today he found on the piano's music rack a volume of Stephen Foster songs, a hint from the management about his repertoire. He acquiesced with a grumble, yet the old, sentimental songs actually brightened the room. One old woman hummed softly out of tune. The applause was more spirited.

In the middle of "Beautiful Dreamer," a shrill, ear-splitting alarm went off inside the house, unnerving those ladies who could hear and abruptly ending the music.

The tall nurse appeared, trying to be calm. "Forgive this interruption. I'll have to ask all our ladies to return to their rooms. We've had a walkaway. We're quite sure it's Georgia Jones. The police have been alerted, but they don't get to our calls very quickly." She turned to Oliver and his grandmother. "Would you two mind helping look for her? We're short-staffed today. She's mobile but very weak. She can't have gotten far."

"Of course," his grandmother declared. "You can certainly count on us. That poor, confused woman."

Outside, the tall nurse took to the sidewalk heading north toward downtown. Another employee headed south. His grandmother pointed him west, toward the river, as she marched off to the east. Oliver felt immense relief to be outside again. Sunlight poured through the ancient elms lining the street. A hotrod screeched around a nearby corner. He pulled off his disgusting tie and unbuttoned his shirt collar. He walked slowly, breathing the sweet air, in sight now of the shining expanse of river. By the time he reached it, he'd mostly forgotten about the woman who'd escaped—that is, until he spotted something white moving in and out of trees near the shore downstream, perhaps someone in a nightgown.

He quickened his step, moved south along the river shore, following the water downstream into thickening woods. The river was broad and slow here. He knew the rapids lay ahead with deep fishing holes just below them. He'd fished those holes with his father on their family visits. They'd caught a few good smallmouth bass.

He came upon a man casting a small silver and red lure with a spinning rod. The man was middle aged—a face Oliver felt he'd seen before—maybe an old school friend of his father.

"Has an old lady come by here?" Oliver asked.

"Haven't noticed." The man glanced at him, and then returned his attention to casting. "Is there a problem?"

"She walked away from the Brown Home."

The man shook his head. "*That* place. Who would blame her? I'll keep an eye out."

Oliver nodded and went on. Some distance ahead he could hear the rush and tumble of the swift, shallow rapids. He began to feel a little afraid for her. Out on the water, an older man drifted by, fishing from a jon boat that could navigate the rapids ahead. The man saw Oliver, waved and smiled. His face was familiar, too. It looked like old Mr. Jarvis, his former fifth grade teacher. But why would he be fishing here when he lived hours away? Still, the weathered face and curly gray hair appeared very like someone he knew.

Seeing no further sign of her, Oliver's sense of urgency diminished. A leaning weeping willow, its roots half in the water, beckoned to him from nearby. He sat down on one of its shoreline roots and watched the water. The river was full of secrets, full of voices. Like the music he played, the water flowed by and was gone-- appearing and disappearing, instantly renewing, forever beginning again. Oliver stared at the moving surface. That the river should change each moment and yet remain the same seemed the deepest of mysteries, beyond his understanding. He noticed a crayfish in a shallow spot among the roots. He reached for it, but it jetted away. Sun and shadows danced on the surface. The water mirrored an image. The reflected face for a moment resembled the old man in the boat, then the middle-aged man with the spinning rod. The distortion cleared, and he saw his own face.

A branch broke somewhere. Oliver glanced downriver—he clearly saw a flash of white disappearing into the trees, so he scrambled to his feet and hurried in that direction. At the spot he had marked mentally, he turned inland. The trees were thick but soon opened up.

He came upon a person in a clearing, a woman sitting on a blanket. She wore a white dress and was taking something from a small basket. She was not the old woman. Oliver was so shocked he cried out "Oh, God! I'm sorry! I didn't mean to disturb you!"

Surprised as well, she smiled and continued putting out what was obviously her lunch. "I think I disturbed *you*."

She was beautiful. He stood gaping at her like a fool.

"You're the boy next door, aren't you? The Wisdoms' grandson?"

Now he recognized her. He managed to find his voice. "Uhh— that's right."

"You've been watching me from an upper window. I've seen you."

His face turned hot. He stammered a bit. "I w-work on my music there. I'm not spying."

"It doesn't bother me. How old are you?"

"Twelve," he admitted reluctantly.

"That's a lovely age. I've been told you're a musical prodigy."

"I'm not sure."

His answer seemed to please her. "Sit down and I'll share my sandwich."

His mouth had gone bone dry. He felt a pulsing in his temples. "I really should keep going. I'm searching for an old lady who ran off from the convalescent home."

"Oh, give her a little freedom. Let her breathe for a while. Sit down and have lunch with me. I'd like to know you better. You remind me of someone."

He stood speechless for several moments and then lowered himself to the ground, facing her. Her dress was a light summer one. It bared her neck and shoulders. Her golden yellow hair spilled down her back and lifted with the slightest breath of wind. Her skirt was full, spread out about her legs. Soft shoes, the sort dancers wear, covered her feet, and her ankles were bare and white.

"Who do I remind you of?" he asked.

"A boy I knew. We were best friends as children. He had the same sweet face and dark curls as you."

"Are you still friends?"

"Well…we got older and fell in love. But my father disapproved of him. We ran away but he caught up to us and took me home again. My friend soon after enlisted in the army and later died in the war. It was all like a story. A bit like Romeo and Juliet."

"A very sad story."

"Yes…much too sad. You're like him. Come closer to me." He did, and she took his chin, leaned into him, and kissed him on the mouth. He'd never been kissed by a girl, let alone a woman. She lingered at it, and he didn't pull away. When she finally leaned back, looking into his eyes, she asked, "Have you ever dreamt of me?"

He was breathless, still recovering, still slightly out of his mind. "I have," he said.

She smiled warmly. "What kind of dreams?"

"I'd rather not say."

"Oh, those kind of dreams." She laughed and kissed him again.

They sat for several moments in silence. She stared at him lovingly.

"I have to go somewhere. I'm so glad I saw you. Stay here and don't follow. It won't take long." She stood, touched his hair with her fingers, and moved away in the direction of the river. He watched her disappear, ghost-like, into the trees. He was confused, full of feeling, wondering what to do. He looked down at her sandwich but had no desire to eat. The moist warmth of her mouth was still on his lips. How desperately he wished to be older. In ten years, the difference between them wouldn't matter. Yet at this moment, time was a tyrant.

When he could not bear waiting any longer, he jumped up and ran to the shore. He looked up and down the river but could see no sign of her. He wanted to call out, but realized he didn't know her name. Upriver, he saw several people coming his way. He moved downriver quickly. At the rapids, the river took a turn and vanished from sight. He hurried in that direction. The rapids were shallow and swift, the river speeding into the bend. When his father and he had fished, they'd waded to the far edge of the swift water and let their lines drift down into the deep holes of the bend. He could see someone standing in that fishing place. He moved closer to the water. He saw clearly that the person was the young woman, her white dress billowing in the current.

"Hello! What are you doing?" he cried out.

At the sound of his voice, she stepped downstream and disappeared beneath the surface. Oliver felt something like a heavy electric shock pass through him. For an instant he couldn't move, and then his legs twitched and began to work. He pushed through the high brush at the water's edge but it thickened until he could not advance. He crashed his way out to the path and ran as hard as he could around the bend. Trying to estimate where she'd be, he saw a fisherman's clearing on the shore and plunged down to it and into the river in his shoes and Sunday clothes. A film of white cloth drifted toward him just beneath the surface. He took a step and the bottom disappeared— he went under in a gasp. Oliver could swim well enough, yet as he grasped the white garment drifting by, her body pulled him downstream like some huge fish he was trying to land. He held on, held his breath for what seemed far more time than humanly possible, until suddenly he felt river bottom again beneath his feet. He rose into the sunlight and madly devoured the air. The fabric in his hand began to rip, so he gathered it toward him, found an arm and then a whole body. He got beneath her and lifted awkwardly. He struggled toward shore, though he found her light as a bundle of sticks. He laid her down in the grass as a policeman arrived, followed by the tall nurse and his grandmother. The policeman and tall nurse examined the limp, bedraggled body in white. The nurse got down on her knees and tried to resuscitate her.

"She's gone," she said at last while Oliver lay exhausted, staring up at a sky full of lacy clouds. "Poor woman. Who'd have guessed she'd had the strength to do it?"

"You were heroic, young man," the policeman said to Oliver.

Oliver looked over and saw the drowned, white-shrouded body of the old woman, Georgia. His grandmother began weeping. She closed her eyes and seemed to be praying.

It was Oliver's first meeting with death, and the weight of it stayed in his arms.

LIGHT AND DARK

Silas watched the sunflower grow from a seed the birds had dropped to a plant towering over his head. A flower broadened at the top, turned bright yellow, and was visited by many small goldfinches nearly the same color. The seeds in the flower head ripened, grew heavy, and the flower bowed down to the overhead sun. The goldfinches began plucking the seeds in rows and flying off to feast on them. Silas's mother tended the garden, his father played scales on the piano in the sitting room, and the world was full of light.

Silas had an older sister, Bess, who was fourteen, tall and bright as a sunflower. He was nearly five years younger, and she sometimes treated him like her own child. Some nights she would read Narnia books aloud sitting beside him in his bed. He loved hearing of the fearsome golden lion with a mane shimmering in the sun. Silas would lean against his sister and watch the soft swelling of her bosom, mysterious and white through the buttoned gaps of her pajamas. Older boys showed great interest in her, and he resented them.

The summer he was twelve, the sunflowers no longer towered over him. He went on a train to visit his grandparents (his mother's parents), who lived in a small fieldstone house near a river just at the outskirts of a farming village. His grandfather was a retired preacher, and his grandmother, a bit younger, still taught piano in their home. Silas's father, years ago, had been her best piano student. Silas's mother had noticed him in his first lesson.

His grandfather had a flowing mane of white hair. He was a stern, quiet man who read most of the time. He mumbled long prayers before meals. Often the food grew cold. Silas wanted to know him better but felt he probably never would.

His grandmother was plump and friendly, talked a bit too much, but loved having a grandson in the house to cook for. Her hair was thick and red like his mother's, with only a touch of grey.

Four days alone with his mother's parents would have been a prison sentence if not for Gracie Pink, who lived just across the road in an aging white farmhouse with red barn and silo. She was older than Silas by a year. The Pink's apple orchards stretched all the way to the river. Gracie was a tomboy who thrived on competitive sports against any boy willing to be beaten. The two of them played basketball in her driveway, and though he was taller, she ran circles around him.

She loved flopping about in their water hole at the river, swinging from a rope tied to a high limb of a massive beech tree and plunging into the water with a shriek. She liked electric trains as much as he did, owned a far better set than his, with villages, bridges crossing rivers, paper mache hills, and multiple tracks on a large plywood table in the basement. He was envious. She allowed him to work the switches but nothing else.

She had chores to do for at least half the day. One of them was to drive their small Farmall tractor through the apple trees with a mower behind. Silas nervously rode beside her, balanced on the narrow fender as she trimmed the wild grass. Her father, who depended on her, had taught her to handle a tractor by the time she was twelve.

Once the mowing was done, they would race down to the river. Silas was fast. Running was the only way he beat Gracie, and that fact seemed to please her. They kept towels and swimming suits on a line tied between two trees. Gracie had no inhibitions about jumping behind a bush and changing clothes. Silas was more self-conscious and went off into the chest-high weeds.

On the day before he was to leave, they raced a final time to the river and quickly changed. Gracie's bathing suit was an old one of her mother's that didn't fit well. She threw herself into the inky river and came up in knee-deep water, her breasts showing through the worn fabric. The legs of the suit fit her loosely, and wispy dark hairs escaped between her thighs. All of this Silas watched with breathless fascination. On the previous two days, he hadn't looked, but now he couldn't help it. She saw his interest, grabbed tight to his wrist and pulled him in. She wrestled him under, and he came up gasping. She climbed on his back and wrapped her legs around him, laughing crazily. She was wiry and strong, and when he tried to shake her off, she gripped him tighter, knotting her feet together. Her heels pressed against the front of his suit, and his unmanageable penis stiffened—as it'd been doing for months, with or without provocation. She rubbed against him with her feet, amused at the touch of it, but finally let go of him. She laughed—a thin, uncertain laugh—and swam to shore, climbed the bank, and reached for the rope swing. He stayed in waist deep water, watching her, his heart thumping wildly.

That night his turbulent thoughts found release for the first time—in sudden, shocking revelation.

That final day of his visit, Gracie and he played basketball in her driveway as though nothing life-changing had happened. Yet the fierceness of her play, the knowing twist of her smile, told him she now possessed some dark power over him. She would haunt his adolescent dreams.

The Petersburg County Fair week marked the near-end of summer. The relentless march of the school year began soon after. Newspapers were full of ads for back-to-school clothing and supplies. Silas hated them, foreseeing the bittersweet end to freedom.

But he loved being with his father's family. They were worlds more interesting than his mother's. His grandfather ran a shoe store in the town of Petersburg. It was reputed to be the best and most modern shoe store in the county. It featured an x-ray machine called a fluoroscope to show parents the fit of shoes on their children's feet. Silas had tried it many times. His grandfather supported the County Fair by leasing the grandstand concession for all of fair week, bringing the family together to work (they nearly always made good money), and hiring local kids to sell refreshments and racing programs in the grandstand during shows that featured harness racing in the afternoons and once-famous entertainers at night.

Silas admired his two uncles, his father's younger bachelor brothers. Billy had been a pilot in the war flying B-29 bombers. In his wallet Silas kept a photo of him in his uniform looking dashing and fearless. The youngest brother Lucas (better known as Lucky), blind in one eye, had stayed home from the war against his will, gone to college, and now wrote for the local newspaper and drove sports cars, often with the town's prettiest girls beside him. Neither was much interested in selling refreshments, so they mainly supervised, told stories, talked to friends, and let Silas, his parents, and Bess run the stand. There was no refrigeration. Bottles of soda cooled in huge corrugated tubs of water with hundred-pound blocks of ice hauled in with sharp tongs by a gaunt, powerful man with leather apron, misshapen shaved head, and several missing fingers.

The county fair was made up of people from two worlds. The majority, comprised of locals (like his family), managed the respectable parts of fair: the animal barns and 4H competitions, the Merchants' Building, the Floral and Exhibition Buildings, and the grandstand concessions and shows. A small but visible minority was made up of a dangerous-looking tribe that set up, tore down, and ran the rides and games, the cheap food booths, the carousel and giant Ferris wheel, the Freaks of Nature sideshow, a Penny Arcade, the Fun House with a Mirror Maze, and a girly show called Raybelles. They were mostly dark, unwashed, hungry-looking men of varied nationalities. They lived in small, battered travel trailers out behind the midway shows. A few, the managers and barkers, wore bright vests and bow ties but still clearly belonged to the tribe. Worn-looking women appeared here and there among them, hanging laundry from lines strung between trailers and occasionally screaming at ragged children in strange languages. It was an alien, menacing world, yet Silas was drawn to it.

On the first day of fair, as they opened the concession stand, a boy, clearly one of that tribe, approached Silas. "How do I get a job here?" he asked. He had an accent that Silas didn't recognize.

He stared at the boy who was somewhere near Bess's age, long-limbed, slender, with shining black hair and huge brown eyes. Silas could not take his eyes off the face that seemed at once young and old, male and female—a face beautiful in a strangely sexless way. His smooth skin was a light olive, his face like a flower.

At that moment, Bess came into the stand, and the boy's full attention went to her. She wore shorts and a county fair tee shirt, her face bright in the morning light. The boy redirected his question to her. She appeared ruffled by his presence and pointed to her uncles just coming into the stand holding cups of coffee. "They're the ones to ask. I don't think we have anything."

The uncles glanced at him, then at each other, and Billy told him no, there were no jobs left. The boy bowed his head politely, smiled, and meandered off, looking back once at Bess.

"I think he likes you," Silas said to her.

"You don't know anything," she snapped back.

On the midway close to where Silas worked, the Raybelles Girls paraded on an outside stage several times a day to advertise the show inside. In previous years, he'd paid little attention, preferring the lively company of his family. Now, he tried not to watch the girls but was drawn like a moth to light. The barker, in red and white stripes and straw hat, spoke with a heavy accent in a loud but musical voice. He introduced each of the girls (hardly girls, though he called them that); they bowed and twirled in turn, energizing gaudy, ruffled costumes that bared long white legs and plump cleavage. The previous night Silas had seen his uncles disappear inside for an evening show. He knew the age to enter was eighteen, no children allowed, yet his imagination came alive with the forbidden things inside that tent.

When he had free time, Silas slipped off alone to the Penny Arcade down the midway from Raybelles. He'd discovered among the games a row of kinetoscope machines that offered two-minute shows for a nickel. One featured a woman in tights standing on a running white horse; another a bird's-eye view of the Grand Canyon; a third a man in a long scarf balanced on the wing of a biplane in flight. The outside of the last machine showed the photo of a dark, sultry woman with painted eyes and the title "Salome – The Dance."

Silas put in a nickel, but the machine didn't come on. He tried another nickel without success.

"I can make it work," someone just behind him half-whispered.

Silas turned to the boy who'd asked for a job the first day of fair. "I'm Fotios. That film gets stuck sometimes because it's watched much more than the others." He moved to the side of the machine and struck a blow with the heel of his hand. "There. Now you can see."

Silas put his face to the viewer. The film was silent, dark and grainy, but Salome twirled to center stage and began (a credit line told him) the dance of the seven veils. He stared in awe. By the end of two minutes, she was dancing naked except for a single veil draped about her hips. A close up showed the veil fall away to darkness an instant before the mystery of her lower body was revealed. Silas raised his eyes from the viewer, shaken, embarrassed to be among people. To his relief, the boy Fotios was gone. He glanced around the room, saw no one looking his way, and struck the side of the machine with his palm. Salome once more began her dance. Silas watched five times, mesmerized by the dancing woman. A familiar hunger grew in him, and he felt a part of himself stepping into a dark place.

He hurried out of the Penny Arcade and back to the stand.   His dear mother had made a pot of chicken soup for all of them; he could smell it above the carnival odors of cotton candy, fried elephant ears, and pronto pups. He ate his fill thankfully, but the hunger remained.

The following afternoon, he saw the boy Fotios again. Silas had carefully avoided the Penny Arcade on his break and gone down the midway to the barns where 4H clubs stalled their horses. A river skirted the fairgrounds, marking the west boundary. It was the same river that he'd swum in with Gracie Pink.

Fotios stood under a large willow overhanging the water. Someone was with him. Silas moved closer and saw, to his shock, that it was his sister Bess. He filled with alarm but didn't dare go up to them. He turned toward the barns, but a moment later he heard Bess calling his name. He looked back and saw her motioning to him.   So he obeyed.

Fotios stood beside her. Bess was smiling brightly. Silas was stunned by the extreme beauty of the two. Bess told him they had met on the shoreline path the day before and become friends. She told him about the boy's Uncle Markos who owned the carnival. She also told him of his Aunt Althea, the fortune teller who had raised and educated Fotios in many arts.

"He's already read my palm," she said.

Fotios responded in a soft voice: "Yes, in her future will be much love, long life. Often those good things don't accompany great beauty. Bess will be fortunate in her path."

"We'll wait and see," she said with a laugh. "What does your own palm say?"

His smile dimmed a little. "Well…I will not be quite as fortunate. How lovely if our paths were tied together, but that isn't the case."

Still full of misgivings, Silas asked, "If your uncle owns the carnival, why did you ask us for a job?"

Fotios took hold of a willow branch and broke it off. "I've watched your family for two years. I wanted to meet you, even work with you since I have a little free time. You're a good family. I wanted to meet Bess. And you, too. You seem to be a young fellow full of curiosity. I know the carnival entices you. If you care to come with me, I'll show you what things are like. I have work to do now, but I can meet you when the afternoon races finish."

"How nice!" Bess exclaimed.

Silas was puzzled at her enthusiasm.

Fotios politely excused himself to return to work. When he was out of earshot, Bess took Silas's hand and whispered, "He is the kindest, sweetest boy I've ever met. Trust him, Silas."

Bess knew boys. She was already a practiced judge of their devious ways. He nodded to her.

So later that day, when harness racing was over, Silas followed Fotios into the carnival. The thin, remarkable boy was dressed as always in loose linen pants and a soft shirt open at the neck. He spoke with a gentle voice, and as he studied the palm of Silas's hand, he told him what he saw. "You are changing from a boy to someone else, and you're excited but troubled."

Silas felt his face and neck flush with embarrassment.

Fotios laughed. "Nothing wrong. It's part of your path. I see unusual things for you, Silas. Your life will be guided by your senses. You'll live more in the world than in the spirit. Women will delight and disrupt your life. You'll create beauty in some way. Is one of your parents artistic?"

Silas frowned at all this and pulled his hand away. "My father's a musician."

"Of course. Your path is to create. It's clear. You'll know joy in moments, but you won't have your sister's happiness. Your life will be harder than hers."

They were walking now among the trailers belonging to the carnival tribe.

"You don't really know these things about me."

Fotios laughed. "I realize it's strange.   I have a gift, but sometimes it's a curse. I've read my own future, as I said before." He laughed again. "And of course that is the curse."

Fotios motioned for him to enter a door at the back of one of the shows. "This is part of the Fun House—we call it the Mirror Maze. Stay with me. I know the way through. The mirrors can be deceivers."

This back lot of the show—full of aging trucks, snarls of heavy electrical cords, and huge, clamoring motors driving the carnival—lay bathed in drab shadow, a bleak scene compared to the bright, garish displays out front. Fotios opened the door with a key and pulled Silas with him.

"Stay by me," Fotios said. "We're entering near the start and others are already in the maze. Remember, the reflections are not you. Some of the mirrors are distorted to startle you. The mirrors confuse illusion and reality so you can't find your way. But, of course, I know the way."

Silas followed him through the door, and it shut behind him. Suddenly, everywhere he looked he saw himself—replicating to infinity. The mirrors made walls invisible, and instinctively he raised his hands to feel his way.

"Mirrors disrupt your orientation," Fotios said in a low voice. "The image in the mirror is reversed. Movements you see are opposite of what you expect. The hallways seem to go on forever in all directions. And the geometry of reflection turns you invisible at moments. It's a puzzle with twists and turns we must find our way through or get lost—" he laughed "—perhaps forever."

"Not funny," Silas said uneasily. He followed Fotios but ran smack into a mirror. He put out his hands to touch it, worked on to the next one, and found himself in a dead end. "Where are you, Fotios?"

"Very near. Put your right shoulder against the glass. Move it to the next glass and the next until you find the exit path."

Silas could see and hear other people nearby him, laughing but trapped as he was. He followed the advice, found the first exit, yet now faced a grotesque vision with a huge head and tiny body. It took him a moment to recognize himself. In a nearby mirror he saw Fotios with head like a pin and body malformed like some human sea creature.

"My true self," Fotios said a laugh.

Silas wasn't amused. "How long does this take?" He heard the fear in his own voice.

"It's your first time in the maze?"

"Yes. I don't really like it."

"The first time can be scary. After that you'll begin to see how mirrors work, showing us ourselves, expanding space and light, revealing the meaning of the maze."

Silas was half listening to him. At the moment he hated the mirrors, wanted only to escape. He felt Fotios take hold of his arm, pull him forward, and suddenly plunge out into the slanting, dust-filled light of late afternoon. They descended the steps of the Mirror Maze and moved onto the midway.

A broad, bear-like man in a barker's striped coat and straw hat came rumbling toward them with a menacing look on his face. "Fotios! Playing around again, you lazy bastard? You know it's time for Dolly."

"I'm going, Uncle Markos," he answered calmly.

Markos glanced at Silas. "Who the hell is this?"

"Just a friend."

"He's a local chump. You know the rule. Get rid of him and get to work."

Markos pointed a crooked finger at Fotios's face and then lumbered off. Silas had seen the man before. He was one of the barkers at Raybelles, the one with the loud, musical voice.

"Come with me," Fotios said. "That swine will never know."

It was the single unkind thing Silas had heard him say.

Silas warily obeyed, following him back toward the public outhouses, foul-smelling buildings that Silas was forced to visit daily. Nearby them stood concrete bathing stalls for horses, the nearest one enclosed by a huge shower curtain.

"Wait here. I'll be only a few minutes." Fotios slipped behind the curtain, and Silas heard a woman's shrieking voice.

"Here you are finally! You're the only one in this show nice to me, but now you're being mean like the others!"

"Forgive me, Dolly," Fotios said gently. "I never want to hurt your feelings. Let me get the water going at the right temperature."

Silas heard water splashing on concrete, followed by a sharp scream and a curse. The woman began to blubber and sob. Silas moved to the edge of the curtain to see. On a heavy wooden bench sat an enormous fat woman, stark naked, whom Fotios was washing down and hosing off like an elephant. She was a mountain of pendulous, drooping flesh. Silas silently backed away and sat down on a stool, feeling dizzy.

"It's too cold, goddammit! You're mean as Markos!"

"So sorry, darling. Is that better?"

She sighed heavily, and in a softer voice said, "Yes, Fotios. Yes, it is."

In ten minutes or so, the water stopped and Fotios emerged, holding an armful of damp towels. "Take these a moment, Silas." Silas reached for them. Fotios lifted a tent-like flowered dress from a peg and carried it inside. Several moments later he was back and took the towels from Silas.

"Is that Dolly Puff? The one from the freak show?"

"It is; she's no freak, though. The show has true freaks. Dolly is only fat. She does it just for the money. There are men who find her attractive. Like Markos."

Silas grimaced. "Honest?"

"Markos has unusual tastes." Fotios shook his head and set off walking back toward the trucks and machinery, carrying the armload of towels. "What do you think of our carnival?"

"I don't know. I'm still learning."

"It's said that when a student is ready, a teacher appears."

"You?"

Fotios smiled. "Yes, maybe. Come in here. I have more laundry to pick up."

They entered a large tent at the rear of one of the shows. It was a dressing room for Raybelles. Silas hesitated, but Fotios motioned him in. Five women sat in the room in various stages of undress. They seemed undisturbed by the presence of the two boys. Each woman was stuffing a cloth laundry bag with costumes and underwear to be washed. The bags were marked with names: Roxy, Glenda, Serena, Flo, Bathsheba. Glenda, a tall, heavy-bosomed redhead, removed her bra and stuffed it in the bag. Her large powdered breasts were bare except for blue circles covering her nipples.

"Fotios is the only one we trust in here," an aging platinum blonde said to Silas. "Are you his friend? If you are, we don't mind. We love him."

They all confirmed that they loved Fotios. Glenda sat down at her mirror, but turned the chair and pulled Silas onto her lap. Silas could smell sweat and strong perfume and feel her heavy breasts against his arm. She hugged him, kissed him on the lips. "Boys are so sweet at this age. Then in a few years they turn into the pigs that come to our shows." The women all laughed at this, Glenda, too, and then she let go of him. Silas flew to his feet, looking pleadingly to Fotios, whose arms were loaded down with towels and laundry bags.

"Help me," Fotios said to him.

Silas took several of the cloth bags and backed toward the exit of the tent. He followed Fotios out and away toward a building where washing was done.

Silas thought about Glenda, the touch and smell of her. She had been too close, too real. He'd sat on her near-naked lap and felt fear instead of hunger.

They both looked back to see Markos, his straw hat in one hand, watching them with half-closed, burning eyes. Silas entered the building behind Fotios, and he dropped the laundry where Fotios indicated.

"You'd better leave soon, but first let me tell you a story," Fotios said, leaning against a wall. "I hate only one man in the world, and he is the one out there watching us. That man, Markos, is not my uncle. Althea is not my aunt, either, though she has sometimes been good to me. Markos abuses her and anyone else he chooses." He paused, as if the next words were painful. "When I was a small child, Markos bought me from my parents."

Silas sat down on a bench, his jaw gaping.

"My parents lived in Greece on a small island. They may still be there. They were very poor. Markos convinced them he could take me to America and help me succeed in life. It was a lie, of course. He used me for his own gain. He's evil—maybe the devil himself. I'll kill him if I ever get the chance."

The frightening assertion cut through Silas like a cold blade. His face drained of blood. For a moment, he was barely able to breathe.

"Forgive me," Fotios said, his kind voice returning. "I didn't mean that. Imagine me killing anyone." He laughed softly.

Silas could not imagine.

Later that night, when Silas had finished working the evening grandstand show, he found himself drawn back irresistibly to the midway. He told his parents he wanted to go on a ride he'd missed, and, as always, they trusted him. He walked by Raybelles. The girls out front were different now, but he felt as if he knew them. The barker was someone else, not Markos. Silas stopped in front of the Freaks of Nature show, studied the gaudy, faded paintings on canvas—of the

Lizard Girl, the Cat Boy, Dolly Puff, the Living Skeleton, the Bearded Lady, the Seal Man, and the special, adults-only attraction, Hermes Aphrodite, the half man, half woman, divided evenly down the middle—the strangest of all. Repulsed by the crude, comic book images, he still paid his quarter and went in. There were two curtained stages, and a doorway to the special show for adults only. A dozen or more people gathered in the viewing area separated from the stages by a three-foot velvet barrier hung on a rope. Silas heard a door close, and a barker appeared from behind one of the curtains. It was Markos.

"Good evening, ladies and gentlemen," he said in his thick accent. "I am Professor Markos. I have spent my life in the study and pursuit of human enigmas. What you will see tonight are flesh and blood human beings who through no fault of their own have come into the world deformed oddities—might we call them the jokes of God? Yet we bring them to you not to laugh or mock, but to educate."

He raised his hand to the right-hand stage and the curtain rose. Dolly Puff sat on a huge, throne-like chair, her pink, sequined dress spread out over her enormous expanse, her legs hanging like Christmas hams, feet not touching the floor. "Displayed here before you is a woman who is more than her prodigious proportions. Her real name is Highness Dolinda Kadare, a deposed Albanian princess whose corpulence was highly prized, even worshipped by her people before the political upheaval in which she lost her family and her title..."

As the story continued, Dolly focused on something above their heads, meeting no one's eyes. Markos invited a second performer to stand beside her. He was a man so emaciated that he was known as The Living Skeleton. Markos, in a raised, tremulous voice, told them that each night the man returned to a graveyard to sleep.

The grim parade continued, Markos narrating the tragic tales of innocent and suffering human beings. Silas often looked away or closed his eyes, wondering why the police hadn't shut down the gruesome display.

With the Seal Man, discovered by a naval military expedition in the Brazilian rain forest, the regular show came to a close.

Yet Markos went on, promising to mature adults a phenomenon so strange that they would never in a lifetime forget it. For a mere twenty-five cents more, anyone eighteen or over could view the eighth wonder of the world, a spectacle unseen by most human eyes, a man and a woman in the same body, the beautiful and famous Hermes Aphrodite. "And yes, ladies and gentlemen," he crowed, "you will see the living proof."

Silas shuddered and stepped into the line, urged on by the gnawing hunger. A tattooed dwarf taking money shook his head. "Not you, sonny boy," he said.

Markos whispered from behind Silas, "Let him in."

The dwarf shrugged and took the quarter from Silas.

Only seven of them from the original crowd followed Markos through the door. Silas found himself facing another stage—set with two short Greek columns made of wood, and dime store vases and urns on which figures of gods and goddesses had been crudely painted. A stage behind the props was curtained and dimly lit. Markos stepped to the front.

"I want to tell you a strange story," he began. "I am Greek, so all of this beautiful ancient culture is dear to me," sweeping an arm to indicate the cheesy props. "Once there was a child born on a small Greek island, a child of Hermes and Aphrodite, the gods of male and female sexuality. The child was winged and like no other on earth. Many, many years later, in my world travels, I found on the same Greek island a direct descendent of that child.

"At great expense, I have arranged to bring her here, wanting to share her with you. Or I should say share *him* with you." Markos paused, peered up at the ceiling of the tent. "To be truthful, ladies and gentlemen, I must leave that for you to decide. With fair warning, then, I present to you the living proof of my confusion, a true wonder of the world, the beautiful, the mysterious Hermes Aphrodite!"

The curtain rose, pulleys squealing. A spotlight wavered, and then settled stage left. A slim, elegant woman emerged with ballet-like movements, her hair black and cascading down her back. She wore a silver sequined dress, shining silver shoes, many bracelets, heavy jeweled necklace, and a black, filmy veil covering all of her face but her eyes. A scratchy recording of bouzouki music filled the tent. The woman began to dance gracefully, weaving about the stage, tossing her flowing skirt and hair. She spun and swirled for the duration of the music and then flung herself onto a green velvet fainting couch near front right stage. The spotlight dimmed.

Silas watched intoxicated as the woman slowly unzipped the front of her dress from the top and opened it, baring small, pointed breasts— breasts like Gracie Pink's. The zipper continued downward until the dress opened fully. She was naked, her legs spread, fully a woman, and—to Silas's horror—a man as well. He stood there unsteadily, heart hammering. The spotlight brightened, gasps rising from the onlookers. Silas tore his eyes away from her lower body to view her face. Round brown eyes were staring directly into his. The curtain fell.

There was no applause, just shattered silence. Silas made a faint mewing sound and lurched toward the exit. Markos was there like a heavy gate. The villain hissed, "Get out of here frightened, fucking little lamb. This world is not yours."

Silas passed by him and ran.

****

Sunday, after they'd been to church, Silas, Bess, their father and uncles returned to the fairgrounds with a pickup truck to clear out their things. The carnival was gone, vanishing in the night, the midway empty except for overflowing garbage cans, broken glass, blowing wrappers. The grass where the shows had stood lay flattened and brown. In a few weeks, though, there would be no sign a carnival had existed.

"I never saw Fotios to say goodbye," Bess said unhappily. "Did you?"

He shook his head.

That winter their grandfather was hospitalized with heart problems, and the family stopped leasing the grandstand concession. Silas went once to the fair the following summer as a spectator, but the carnival was a different one, without a girly show or freaks.

Nonetheless, his memory of Fotios remained—indelible. Nor could he erase (hard as he tried) the dark words of Markos, "Get out of here, frightened, fucking little lamb. This world is not yours."

Silas, over time, learned otherwise.

MEAN LITTLE BLOSSOM PEAVY

There was a child named Blossom Peavy who often disturbed her family and her third-grade teacher because she didn't hem and haw when she spoke up. Her mother Rita was pretty in a dime-store kind of way, and not very smart about anything. Her two older brothers were dimwits, and her grandmother was critical of them all. Unfortunately, they were forced to live with her because Blossom's father had deserted them and taken the money. He drove Greyhound buses cross country, and one day kept going. Blossom hardly knew him.

The grandmother had enrolled them in a Baptist school, feeling that would whip them into shape. Blossom's teacher, Mrs. Crow, read them stories about Jesus nearly every day. Blossom raised her hand one afternoon and said, "Why do we read about Jesus so much? Let's read about someone interesting, like Bilbo Baggins." Another time, she told Mrs. Crow, "That's not a nice dress. It looks like wallpaper."

Mrs. Crow was exasperated by Blossom, who knew more about Charles Dickens, black holes, and Plato's Allegory of the Cave than she herself ever would. Blossom rocked endlessly in her seat as if dying to run off. Yet when called on, she delivered detailed, accurate, if not entirely coherent answers. She was rude to classmates without meaning to be. When one of them fumbled with a math problem on the board, she would say with no mockery intended, "Goodness sake, it's so easy." If one of them wouldn't share, she'd refuse to play, take her toys, and go off by herself. For such things she became known as Mean Little Blossom Peavy. She disliked being touched, even by her mother. She had no friends, but that didn't seem to upset her. On the swings she would pump as high as possible, imagining flying away like a bird.

Blossom loved solitude but hadn't found much of it in their tiny bungalow back in Birdseye, Indiana. Her parents took the single downstairs bedroom, her brothers the upstairs dormer, with Blossom stuck in the hallway at the top of the stairs just off the dormer. The oxen brothers rumbled through her space coming and going every day. She carefully lined up pencils and schoolwork on her small desk, and one of the two (Buddy was four years older, Fred two) often scattered her things just to hear her shriek. Her single escape was the library next door. Though a stone-faced lady librarian questioned the age appropriateness of the books she chose, the place had few people and a lovely, enforced quiet.

Her grandmother's house was larger and much older than the house in Birdseye. Maude Hightower had lived there her entire marriage, raised three children who, when they were old enough, had moved as far away as they could get. Her husband, owner of the Hightower Department Store, had died suddenly in his early fifties and left her a business she soon found to be mired in debt. She had believed they were wealthy people, and discovering otherwise had given her already sour disposition an acid edge.

The boys had an attic room to themselves, and Blossom shared an upstairs bedroom with her mother, who had adenoid problems (from second hand smoke in the bar where she waitressed) and snoring problems as a byproduct. Some nights Blossom would bury her head in pillows, trying to escape the bulldozer sounds from across the room. The peaceful public library was downtown, miles away, so Blossom sometimes felt that, day and night, she was drowning in a tidal wave of noise.

That went on until one unusual morning, the very first day of her summer break. It was the morning she found Raspberry Books.

That morning had started badly. Blossom's grandmother, who had never approved of Luke Peavy, said to Rita, "I always told you that so-called husband of yours was no good, and he has certainly proved me right. Peavy…it's a white trash name. Highbridge is so much more dignified. Rita Peavy…" She whined it through her nose. "Honestly, it sounds like a squeaky door…a frightened little mouse. You should change it back."

Rita stared down at her coffee. "It's my name, mother. Don't make them think it's low class." By "them" she meant her three children sitting at the table eating Cheerios.

"You dropped out of college because of that man. Now you're nothing but a waitress. He was the ruin of you, Rita. You were never smart about men or much else for that matter. Your children are certainly testimony to it. Blossom is a case. I've talked to my pastor about her. He thinks she's on the spectrum."

Blossom's mother got up and quietly left the room so they wouldn't see her tears. Buddy and Fred finished their Cheerios in silence. They still had tests to take before school ended for them. Fred was working on math with a dazed look. Blossom glanced at his worksheet. It was long division.

"You're doing it wrong," she said.

"You don't know anything about it," Fred grumbled.

"It's only dividing five digits by one digit. The answer to this one is 154, the answer to this is 270…your answers are wrong."

Buddy pushed his empty cereal bowl to the center of the table and grabbed the worksheet. "I hate it when you do that, Stinkblossom." He stared at the paper. "Yeah, hers are right, yours are wrong, bone-head."

"Goodness sake, I can do the problems in my head," Blossom said in a factual manner.

"Shut up, goddammit!" Fred shouted and left the room, slamming the door.

Blossom was baffled and amazed at his behavior.

"Now look what you've done," her grandmother said, shaking a bony finger.

"Nice going, little sister," Buddy said.

"What's wrong with him, anyway?"

"You're so clueless, Blossom."

"Cold as a stone," her grandmother added. "No feelings at all."

"I have lots of feelings," Blossom answered. *Too* many, she decided, as she watched the rest of her family leave the room. She finished her Cheerios alone, wrote a note saying "I am on a walk," and then went out in a direction she'd never taken.

Raspberry Books appeared as a lovely surprise, only three blocks from her grandmother's house on a corner just south of Oriole Street. It was old, slate grey and ornate, full of decorative trim painted in pinkish mauve and dark green. An arched trellis of honeysuckle served as entranceway. At the top of the trellis hung a sign that read RASPBERRY NEW AND USED BOOKS. WELCOME. Flagstone paths led to a wide front porch lined with rocking chairs. The paths also branched off to the left around the house and into back acreage of loosely organized gardens of flowers, vines, herbs, hedges, and many, many old trees.

Blossom walked under the arched trellis, wondering if she were still asleep and dreaming. No one sat on the porch, and when she climbed the steps and tried the front door, she found it locked. A sign told her the bookshop opened at 9 a.m. She guessed the time was around 8:30. As she turned to leave, the door swung wide, and a very thin woman with keen, gleaming eyes and white-gold hair pulled into a messy bun stood smiling at her. She wore a flowing black skirt and a red body suit. Her feet were bare.

"Hello, there," she said in a singsong voice. "It's early, but would you like to come in? I'm Miss Raspberry. I've made tea."

Blossom, wide-eyed, followed her in. They passed through two rooms with floor to ceiling books. Above a stairway in the corner hung a sign reading USED BOOKS, with an arrow pointing up. Blossom followed her through a door into an old-fashioned kitchen with lino-leum counters. On a small round table sat a teapot wrapped in a cloth cozy of quilted birds. She pulled out a chair, Blossom sat, and Miss Raspberry poured her tea. "Do you like cream and sugar?"

"Yes, cream and three sugars."

Miss Raspberry nodded. "I've told you my name. What is yours?"

"Blossom Peavy."

"Well, Blossom, do your parents know you're here?"

"My mother does. I left her a note. We live just down the street with my grandma."

"How old are you?"

"Nine. Almost ten."

"That's a wonderful age. Ten was my favorite year. Are you here to buy a book?"

"I don't have any money. But I love books."

"No matter about money! What do you read?"

"Oh, science and history and intelligent fantasy. I like Victorian novels, especially Dickens, although Jane Eyre is my favorite character."

Miss Raspberry brightened. "Oh, mine too! What a wonderful coincidence! Jane Eyre is so strong—so misused by family and school authorities and yet so whole and…and true to herself. My, your reading level is mature for your age. You seem quite special. When we finish our tea, I'd like to show you my garden if you'd be interested. Then I'll open the bookshop and you can browse all you want, inside and out."

So after tea they wandered back to Miss Raspberry's garden, a place she described to Blossom as wildness loosely contained. "It leans toward the unkempt," she said with a small laugh, "but I love the green magic of it. I'm a bit of a Transcendentalist. Do you know that word?"

"I think so."

"Well, I feel a spirit in the garden—God in His most refined form, his clearest incarnation. I feel peace and harmony and wholeness here. And at certain rare moments I become part of it all."

Ordinarily, when people talked about feelings, she didn't listen. But now, as she wandered the flagstone path with this odd woman, among crabapple trees dressed in white and pink, big-shouldered mounds of deep purple lilac, fat poppies with bursting orange faces, she felt a glimmer.

Her grandmother, pounding chicken breasts with a tenderizer hammer, said, "Lucinda Raspberry has bats in her belfry."

Blossom's mother, who had visited the bookshop and talked to Miss Raspberry about Blossom working in her gardens (and being paid in books), replied, "She's a little strange but I like her. It'll give Blossom a good way to spend some time this summer. Miss Raspberry thinks she's very special."

"That *is* strange. Well...I suppose the woman is harmless enough." Maude Hightower said this in a manner quite mild for her. "At least the child won't be underfoot as much. I was wondering how I'd manage with her the entire summer. I approve the plan."

"How nice of you, mother. I've already told her yes."

Blossom was surprised and pleased at her mother's assertiveness. Her grandmother scowled but sealed her curling lip.

And thus began a summer unlike any other of Blossom's short life. Weeding did little to inspire her, but the delicate routine of deadheading—the pots and window boxes of flowers, petunias especially—brought her great satisfaction. She worked, often alongside Miss Raspberry, with small garden scissors, cutting at the exact place on stems to urge more blooms. Nature was so much more companionable than people. It thrived on careful attention, which Blossom happily gave. She watered and fertilized whenever the need arose. Her flower family responded and multiplied.

Except for birdsong and a murmur of traffic on Oriole Street, Miss Raspberry's garden was blessedly quiet. Though she liked Miss Raspberry quite a lot, she liked the garden better. A small grotto with a wicker chair, surrounded by tall cedars, was the place she liked most to read her books. Nearby was a birdbath where squirrels came to drink and birds to splash. Earned by her own labor, the first book she chose was a used copy of *Treasure Island*. She found it thrilling if a bit long-winded and difficult. The second was *The Secret Garden*, which she loved because of Mary, the outspoken main character, and Dickon, the wild boy, who befriended birds and other small creatures.

She thought she might become friends with the chipmunks and squirrels and birds and even occasional rabbits who visited daily. She was quiet and patient. The early June explosion of tulips, forget-me-nots popping wherever they pleased, peonies in great pink and white puffs, drifts of lilies of the valley and purple dragon, soon gave way to Asian lilies in yellow, pink, and orange, to clematis in tangles of darkest purple. In the middle of the garden, a pond with goldfish reflected the garden, the sky, the passing clouds. Blossom looked to Miss Raspberry for names of everything and worked hard to remember. In a sketchbook she did pencil drawings of the living things she observed, learning the garden in detail.

Miss Raspberry's father appeared one day, surprising her. He was aged and rotund, a bit like Old Fezziwig, but smarter and more serious. The two Raspberrys, she'd learned, lived in the back part of the house, separated from the bookshop. He walked with a cane but still helped in the shop some days and knew books even better than his daughter.

Blossom was upstairs choosing a book from the used section when she discovered Mr. Raspberry standing beside her. "Try this one," he said, handing her a copy of *Through the Looking Glass* by Lewis Carroll. "Lucinda tells me you're an unusual child. This is an unusual book." It was the first he'd talked to her, and she was surprised.

"Thank you," she told him.

"Come. I want to show you something."

He took her to a blue wall containing an antique photograph of a plain young woman with dark hair pulled back and a mole above her right eye. "Do you know who this is?"

"I've seen her in a book, I think."

"It's Emily Dickinson," he said, glancing at Blossom. "She's Lucinda's favorite poet—a very eccentric lady but a genius. Emily needed to be alone most of the time because people, especially in groups, caused her anxiety. She became so overwhelmed by certain beloved presences that she had to speak to them through a closed door."

"Too many feelings," Blossom said.

"So you *know*," he answered and smiled. He reached and pulled a book from a shelf beneath the picture. "Lucinda says you're a very good gardener. I want you to have this extra book as a gift. These are some of Emily's poems."

She accepted it with an intake of breath.

Later that day, Blossom sat in the grotto reading a small poem about a bird. It began in this way:

A bird came down the Walk-
He did not know I saw-
He bit an Angle Worm in halves
And ate the fellow raw…

And then, he drank a Dew
From a convenient Grass-
And then hopped sideways to the wall
To let a beetle pass-

Blossom's cheeks warmed. So charmed was she by the odd singularity of "a Dew" and "a convenient Grass" (as if she were meeting each by itself), that she wished very much she could be friends with this poet, just as she wished to be friends with Jane Eyre.

At home, though, things seemed to be coming apart. During dinner one night, Buddy had a riddle for them. "Where does a fish keep his money?"

No one answered.

"In a river bank!" he crowed triumphantly.

His mother smiled faintly.

"Nobody told me that. I made it up myself. Mr. Hurt said I was very clever."

Her grandmother snorted. "You nearly flunked his class, for heaven's sake. If you're clever, you're a clever numbskull."

Buddy's smile faded.

"Then he's an oxymoron," Blossom said.

"Never call me a moron, Stinkblossom." He held up a clenched fist.

"I didn't."

"She honestly didn't, Buddy," her mother said, trying to help.

The grandmother glared at Blossom. "Don't use words you don't understand, little Miss Peavy. An oxymoron is...is a figure of speech...umm, an exaggeration."

"That's hyperbole," Blossom said quietly. "Oxymoron is a union of opposites—like when you called Buddy a clever numbskull."

Her grandmother's face turned a deep shade of red. "Don't contradict me, young lady."

"I'm not. I'm correcting you."

Maude Hightower next turned puce. Blossom was puzzled and a bit anxious. "Your face is very red, grandma. It's ugly like that."

"Go to your room!" she shrieked.

Shocked, Blossom hurried away, the house still trembling as she shut the bedroom door.

A miraculous thing happened on a morning in late June as Blossom read *Through the Looking Glass* snuggled down in the wicker chair. Alice had already stepped through the glass into a world in which everything was backward, including logic. Blossom had read the start of the Jabberwocky poem by holding it over the pond and reading the reflection. It was wonderfully clever and utterly bizarre. As she went on reading, a very small chickadee, one she'd noticed close by before, alighted on the arm of her chair. It shocked her. Blossom held her breath and stopped reading. The quick little bird hopped near to her book and seemed to be trying to study it.

The bird stayed there, making soft little chits and tweets.

"Oh, my," Blossom said in her very softest voice.

In return she heard a soft "Fee-bee, fee-bee," from the bird.

"I wish I could fly," Blossom whispered.

The small, wild thing seemed to be studying her now. Blossom found this amazing and delicious. A breeze picked up a corner of one page, and the chickadee flew off, but perched on the nearby birdbath and dipped in for a drink.

"I'll be your friend," Blossom whispered, as blessed as she'd ever felt.

The bird answered, "Fee-bee."

Miss Raspberry was pleased at this news but not at all surprised. "Chickadees are very social. It's probably a young one. You should give him a name."

"It's a boy, I'm sure. I'll call him Fee Bee because that's who he says he is."

And it was, as it turned out, a bosom friendship. Fee Bee was the first to the feeder every morning, waiting for Blossom to fill it. His chits and tweets, Blossom knew, were Chickadee words for "Good morning, my friend." Blossom wondered what she'd done to earn the affection of this small wild creature, but she knew she loved him more than anyone or anything. She didn't mention Fee Bee even once to her family.

And on one special day, Blossom put six sunflower seeds into the palm of her hand and held them out. Fee Bee watched, hopping from birdbath to chair and back for several minutes, and next held rigidly still, as if thinking. All at once, he burst upward, and alighted like a feather on Blossom's hand. He took a seed and soared off to a branch to crack it. Blossom was bewitched. She was too full of love to speak. Fee Bee returned to her hand for another seed. "Fee-bee," he said to Blossom as if now the matter was settled.

Blossom began carrying her lunch in her school lunchbox so she wouldn't have to go home at noon. She often ate in the garden with Fee Bee busy nearby. Some days Miss Raspberry invited her to the kitchen to share lunch with her, always with tea, while her father watched the shop. They usually talked about books, and Miss Raspberry told her several times that she enjoyed books much more than people. Blossom nodded, understanding. Miss Raspberry once spoke of her dead grandfather Elias Raspberry who founded the bookshop.

"He visits me now and then, and we talk about business," she said in a half-whisper. "He believes I should stock more thrillers and mysteries. I tell him I don't want crowds of the wrong people in my shop. Just a few true lovers of good books. I'm sure you understand."

Blossom nodded and drank her tea. She sensed Miss Raspberry wanted to be a closer friend.

Another day, Miss Raspberry took her to an inside drawing room with dark mahogany walls, a large fireplace and mantle with massive mirror above—a room overfilled with brittle-looking antique furniture. Three dollhouses stood on tables in different parts of the room. They were full of miniatures of families dressed in the clothing of what looked to be Victorian times, with furniture from the period. The precision of their placement—a woman standing at an open door, a child on a rocking horse, a baby in a cradle, a man at a desk—touched a chord in Blossom, as if in this careful order she could read Miss Raspberry's mind.

"These are my families," Miss Raspberry said sweetly. "I rearrange them several times a week." She laughed quietly. "I keep them well dressed and comfortable. We have fun. In return, they mind me very well."

Blossom looked up at the mirror above the fireplace and wondered if Miss Raspberry ever visited the other side of it.

Blossom's mother had gone out twice with Jack, the man who owned the bar where she worked. Blossom's grandmother was livid.

"You aren't even divorced yet, you foolish girl!" she snapped.

Rita Peavy turned her back and refused to listen. It was a new tactic, and it confused the witch. Blossom worried about it, fearing her mother would do something to jeopardize the fragile stability of her life at Raspberry Books. Buddy and Fred were both on Little League teams and stayed away much of each day. On Sunday, their grandmother went to her Baptist church alone. Their mother went out the moment she'd left, most likely to meet the bar owner. The boys played baseball in a vacant field nearby, and Blossom read on the back porch, since Raspberry Books closed every Sunday. But her mind spun as she mostly stared at words.

That week, over lunch with Miss Raspberry, their friendship took a turn. As they chatted about *Oliver Twist*, which Blossom had just read, she noticed a large manila envelope resting beside Miss Raspberry's teacup. They went on talking as Blossom's curiosity rose.

"What is that?" she asked at last.

"This? Funny you should mention it. I write, you know."

"I didn't know."

"Yes. It's a short book for young adults. You aren't a young adult yet, but you're an old soul and read more perceptively than most adults I know. You are amazing to me. You remind me of myself. I would be honored if you would give me your opinion. I've sent it to a few book people we know but haven't heard back yet. They're very busy."

Blossom felt a touch of apprehension, something she rarely experienced. Once in the spring Buddy had asked her to read something of his, and his writing, not surprisingly, was illiterate. Fred struggled with numbers, Buddy with words. A book she could read in a day would take him a month, and then he couldn't remember it. He'd resented her comments on his small, stupid essay about breaking in his baseball glove. All she'd done was tell him the truth, and for a week or more he'd hated her for it.

Miss Raspberry, fortunately, was not Buddy. But her manuscript seemed a dense weight on her lap as she opened the envelope in the garden. She read the title *Little People* by Lucinda Finch Raspberry. She read the first line, "At night, when the moon was full, the dollhouse people began to move about." To her relief, the line aroused her interest, though something about it worried her. The thin, ninety-page book took her an hour and a half to complete. She could not, in all her reading life, recall a duller story.

Blossom returned the manuscript to its envelope. Miss Raspberry, who had been watching from a window, appeared within minutes.

"Oh, I'm all aflutter," she chirped, standing in front of Blossom. "What did you think, my dear?"

Blossom hesitated, cleared her throat, looked around for moral support from Fee Bee, but her friend was nowhere in sight. "Well, having dollhouse people come to life is a very interesting idea."

Miss Raspberry pressed her hands together. "I thought you'd think so."

"But your little people are happy from beginning to end. They don't have any problems."

"Yes, that's right. That was my intent. It's what makes the book unique. The lady who owns the miniatures creates a happy, benevolent world for them, like a loving God. I believe children need to feel that life is safe and happy."

"But it isn't," Blossom said.

Miss Raspberry was taken aback but recovered in a breath or two. "How did you like it overall?"

"Not very much."

Miss Raspberry's skin lost its color. Her face sagged like an undercooked cake. Blossom was about to say how ugly she looked, but thought better of it. Several silent, anxious moments went by before Miss Raspberry bent and lifted the manila envelope from Blossom's lap. Her smile was polite. "Well, I'm still working on it. Thank you for your time and comments. I hope the next draft will please you more." She hurried up the flagstone path to the house, where Mr. Raspberry watched from a window.

For the first time in her life, Blossom wondered about the wisdom of doing what she'd always done—telling the truth. Was there anything more important than truth? She couldn't think of a thing, but still she wondered.

At eleven the next morning, with Fee Bee perched atop her lunch box, Blossom heard her name being called and looked up to see her mother marching down the flagstone path toward her. Fee Bee disappeared into the trees in a flash of white and black.

"Get your lunchbox, Blossom," she said breathlessly. "We're going away."

"Going away where?"

"A new home. I can't stand this a second longer."

"But I can't leave this garden, mother. I need to be here."

"You're my daughter, Blossom. You go where I go. I'm sorry, but that's the way it has to be."

Their ramshackle car was waiting in front of the bookshop, loaded with brothers, suitcases, boxes, baseball equipment—everything. Her mother wouldn't wait five minutes for her to speak to Miss Raspberry.

Blossom sat in back atop a suitcase. Her life was ending. Her heart already ached for Fee Bee, the one kindred spirit she had ever known. Never had it ached before, and the pain was causing earthquake-like fractures inside her. The hurt was too intense….and why now, she agonized, after all the years of not feeling it? At that moment, she wanted to die.

But of course she went on living.

Jack's cottage was a termite-infested shack on a small, crowded lake forty-five minutes from town. He was lending it to them for the cost of utilities. It had plastic wrap storm windows and a small space heater. They'd never last the winter in it.

On her birthday in August, Blossom's mother drove her into town and dropped her at Raspberry Books with money to buy whatever book she wanted. She went into the shop before visiting the garden. Miss Raspberry greeted her coolly, saying she was surprised she'd left without notice.

"My mother moved us away. I never had a chance to tell you. How is Fee Bee?"

"Oh, I'm sure he's fine. I don't know him like you do. You're welcome to wander the garden to see. He might be off looking for a mate, though."

"I have money to buy a book. It's my birthday."

Miss Raspberry smiled more warmly. "So now you're ten. How wonderful."

Blossom took a risk. "Is your book coming along?"

"Oh, I've decided to give it up. You were right. What is life or art without problems? I'm best running a bookshop."

Blossom bought a newly published book Miss Raspberry recommended, *Harry Potter and the Sorcerer's Stone*, and later sat an hour in the garden reading, but Fee Bee never came.

Before she left to meet her mother, Blossom saw Mr. Raspberry wandering slowly out, using his cane.

"Hello, young lady," he said, quite winded. "I wanted…well, I wished to tell you how brave you are—braver than I. I'm beholden to you." He touched the top of her head, and turned back toward the house. Blossom sat mystified.

Blossom's mother moved them again before winter. In the space of two months, she'd learned to hate Jack the bar owner and had found another job two hours north. They lived in a drafty cabin in the woods, and Rita worked scheduling medical appointments from an office thirty miles away. Her hours were long, and she had little time to clean or cook. The three kids took a bus to public school and got home the last of anyone. The boys still struggled with learning. Blossom helped whenever they'd let her, but they much preferred their Mortal Kombat video game. On nights when her mother ended a shift exhausted, Blossom began making them grilled cheese and sometimes tomato soup. She cleaned up the kitchen afterwards.

One evening close to Christmas, as Blossom and her mother fashioned tacky crepe paper ornaments for a tree the boys had cut in the woods, her mother for no apparent reason took her tightly into her arms and wept—wept until the boys looked up from Mortal Kombat in puzzled irritation.

Blossom didn't push away.

HARRY AND DOROTHY

Harry stood in the graveyard of the First Methodist Church staring down at his uncle's coffin as a preacher with sagging, barnacled face spoke so slowly and deliberately that Harry doubted the man would live to the benediction. To his left, rippling in the midafternoon August heat, lay the four-block business district of Gulch City, Kansas. To his right stretched the broad, flat fields of wheat and corn reaching to the edge of sky, and scattered grasslands, remnants of the prairie, baking to a gray mass in the sunlight. The only color in the scene was Harry, who wore bellbottom jeans and a loose, brightly flowered linen shirt in shades of purple and yellow. His dark hair was shoulder-length, and his beard raggedly trimmed. He wore large, green-rimmed sunglasses. Mourners around him were uneasy, wondering if Lucas Hill's nephew, an ordained preacher, had somehow turned into a hippie.

Harry hadn't been back to Gulch City (excepting for parents' funerals) since his eighteenth year, when he'd escaped to a college in Indiana. He'd partied hard, later found God, entered a seminary, become the pastor of a small Indiana church, from which he'd recently been banished for heretical thinking. Jobless for some time, too old to be drafted, he'd read Kerouac and taken to the road, buying and selling dried psilocybin mushrooms when the opportunity arose, and sitting in now and then with rock 'n' roll bands.

Harry had not the faintest desire to return to his birthplace--until he found, as his uncle's only heir, that he now owned a Kansas farm. He glanced around at the group of fellow mourners. Faces here and there were vaguely familiar, but sun and wind and twenty-five years had turned most of them into pieces of the landscape, parched and cheerless.

Yet as he glanced about, he noticed one with a difference, a woman in a red hat, red shoes, and faded gingham dress, standing apart from the others. He stared at her, trying to remember. Her eyes were downcast, but her auburn hair and flushed cheeks brought back the dim memory of a girl in high school, someone a year or two younger than he was. Dorothy, was it? Dorothy something or other. She'd been unusual in some way that had attracted attention.

"Lord of all," the pastor droned on, "we commend Lucas Marlin Hill...er, Lucas Marvin Hill into your loving arms. May he rest in peace, and..." A wind blew the pages of his liturgy and with them his place. "...rest in peace...in plenty of peace...and bless this food to our use. Amen."

The crowd repeated "amen," and the interminable service ended. Several men stopped to shake Harry's hand. One heavy man in bib overalls and a black sport coat nodded and said, "It's a good farm. You don't look much like a farmer."

"Amen to that," Harry said cheerfully. "I'm a preacher at present, but looking for a change in my life. Maybe this is it." In truth, he planned on selling the farm as fast as he could and disappearing out west somewhere, out of the reach of troubles closing in on him.

"Don't look much like a preacher, neither," the man said, moving away.

Harry sat for a while on the front steps of the church in the shade, thirsty for a beer. He had been invited to a gathering at a neighbor lady's house for cake and coffee. He didn't know her and had no desire to go--but felt nudged by a vague sense of duty. With a weary sigh he stood and made his way toward his battered Volkswagen bus, taking a shortcut through the graveyard.

Dorothy remembered Harry Hill, even though she'd only spoken to him once or twice in high school. She'd been a daydreamy, unpopular sophomore; he was top of the pecking order, basketball star, fancy dancer, guitar player, brainy senior with a wild streak that charmed the girls. When she'd heard years later that he'd become a preacher, she could only think that God had worked a miracle.

As she planted pots of Shasta daisies at the gravestones of the uncle and aunt who'd raised her, she noticed Harry coming in her direction. She kept planting, only looking up when she felt him standing over her.

"Dorothy?" she heard him say. She put down her trowel.

"How are you, Harry?" She looked up at him. He grinned and took off his green sunglasses.

"Been a long time," he said.

"You've changed."

"I would hope so." He went silent for several moments; she shrugged and resumed digging. "Is family buried here?" he asked.

She nodded toward the headstones. They read "Henry Allen Gale, 1898-1965. Emily Marie Gale, 1900-1966."

"The farm is mine now," she told him. "I have a man to help, but I lease most of the land."

"Dorothy Gale. Now I remember."

"It's Dorothy Green nowadays."

"Of course. You'd be married."

"Divorced. What about you?"

"Never gotten around to either one."

"That surprises me. So does the look of you. More technicolor than I expected."

He smiled and sat down on the grass. "You coming for coffee and cake?"

"No. I'm not very social."

"Too bad. I was hoping for company. Hardly know a soul."

She finished the planting and stood, removing her gardening gloves. "Your uncle's land butts up to mine. He was leasing one of my fields for alfalfa."

He got to his feet, towering over her by a whole head. "I guess that makes us neighbors." He stared down at her, making her uneasy.

"What is it? Why you looking at me like that?"

"There was an odd thing about you that I'm just trying to remember…"

She laughed sharply. "Odd is the right word. It's always been. Some people here even say I'm a witch because of being an herbalist. I grow and sell my own natural herbal medicines and health products— with no eye of newt or toe of frog in my formulas. They buy from me in spite of the rumors. I'm also a storm chaser part time."

"Hmm…fascinating. But I'm referring to something when you were young. Maybe something about dreams and visions."

She gave him a weary glance. "I should get on home now."

"Wait. I'd like to talk a little more. I'm very into dreams and visions. Need a ride?"

"I have transportation, thank you."

He watched her pack her trowel, gloves, and pots into a basket and head off toward an old Ford pickup truck. She climbed up into it and drove off, not looking his way. He felt disheartened and grew more so when he found the battery of his VW bus stone dead. Cake and coffee obligations left him. He leaned down and pulled out a blue cloth bag hidden beneath the dashboard, quickly stuffing it in his left cowboy boot. A big black leather Bible sat on the passenger seat. The back of the bus had been fitted out with a camp mattress and sleeping bag. Clothes hung here and there, covering the side windows. Books were stacked about, and two guitars, one acoustic, one electric, tucked in corners. Harry took a partially drunk beer from a cooler and finished it in a swallow. He got out, locking the door and kicking it shut, looked angrily down the dusty road that led to his farm, and set out walking. "Damn pile of junk," he muttered. He saw the late afternoon sun perched at the tip of the First Methodist steeple like a fat, luminous Buddha. Before he'd walked a half mile, his flowered cowboy boots had begun to pinch.

From down the road Harry heard a siren, then spotted a state police car speeding toward him. He stepped into the corn field and knelt down until the car and dust had disappeared. As he moved out of the crisp cornstalks, he saw a white van coming from the other direction. He stayed to the side of the road and let it pass. But it didn't pass. The van slowed, then pulled to the side, and a shiny bald head poked out the driver's window. A dust cloud followed, billowed over the van, and went its way. Harry could read letters on the van spelling out GREEN'S PHARMACY. FREE DELIVERY.

"Need a ride, mister?" the bald head called out. Harry waved, quickened his pace and finally broke into a run. His feet were feeling raw. He threw open the passenger door, but the seat was filled with small white paper bags.

"The back seat is clear. Use the slider."

Harry did just that and shook the extended hand of a tall scarecrow of a man in a white pharmacist's coat and round wire glasses. "Bevel Green. Where you headed?"

"Going just up the road to my uncle's farm. I'm Harry Hill."

"Hmmm, you're Luke Hill's heir. Don't look a whole lot like a preacher."

"I own a suit, but the day was too hot."

"Smart-looking sunglasses, though. I got just one stop-off to make before your uncle's place. Won't take but a moment." Within a mile he pulled into the yard of a small, paintless farmhouse. Behind it was an acre or more of carefully tended garden and a small barn leaning precariously.

"Who lives here?"

"My ex-wife."

"You said your name's Green?"

"Says so on my van."

"Then it's Dorothy Green lives here."

"That's right. We're split up, but we still do some business together. An amicable divorce, you might call it."

"Mind if I come in with you? I knew her way back in high school."

Bevel shrugged. "Suit yourself."

The two of them went up the steps of the front porch to the door. Two red chickens sat in the two rocking chairs. A scruffy black dog raised his chin from a shady spot under a porch swing, lowered it again and closed his eyes. Bevel knocked once, and then opened the door. Dorothy looked up from the kitchen counter where she was working.

"Almost ready, Bevel. Come on in while I get it all in a box." She noticed Harry coming in just behind her ex-husband. "You again."

"I was walking, and Bevel was kind enough to pick me up along the way. My battery died."

"Well, I'll drive you the rest of the way, and Bevel can get on with his deliveries."

The two men sat at a plank table while she packed small jars into a box.

"I sell Dorothy's herbs and essential oils for steam inhalation. Also, her skin products. Very popular items with my customers. I scratch her back, she scratches mine, so to speak. What sort of church did you preach in, Harry?"

"Baptist. Small congregation of conservative older folks. After a time, we didn't see eye to eye theologically, unfortunately. These days I tend toward theologians like Emanuel Swedenborg and Timothy Leary. My ideas have changed because of certain visions I've been blessed with."

"Not familiar with those names. Billy Graham is my personal choice. This is good conservative country, too."

"Oh, I know," Harry said. "I grew up here. I was pretty wild back then, Bevel, until God reached out and took ahold of me. No telling where I'd be today without God taking me hard by the scruff of the neck."

"Well, hallelujah to that."

"Praise God, is what I say."

"Praise God, brother."

"Here's all of it," Dorothy said to Bevel. "And your invoice."

Bevel stood, took the box from her, shook Harry's hand, and went out. She sat down across from Harry, where Bevel had been.

"We used to live above the pharmacy in town. He still lives there. He's a knucklehead, but I need him for business."

Harry scratched his beard at the jawline. "I can't see you married to him."

She hesitated a moment. "I'd known a certain amount of adventure before I met him. He'd get excited by the color in my stories and promised we'd make our own stories, meaning travel to faraway places, and he also promised children." She was puzzled why she was telling her personal life to a near-stranger, but his interested green eyes and his uncommon presence encouraged it. She went on. "None of it ever happened, of course. He wasn't what he made himself out to be. The business took all his energy. Not ever enough time or money to see the wider world. He got viewing everything in black and white like other folks around here. Then he got himself fixed without telling me." She felt her face heat up. "It was the final straw. My uncle and aunt had died, and I moved in here."

"Now that's real deceitful of him." He shook his head in disbelief and looked at her with sympathy. "And here you are by yourself, no husband, no kids. Kind of lonely, isn't it?"

"Doesn't bother me. You're more company than I'm used to."

She shut up then, called the dog inside, and drove Harry a mile or two up the road to his uncle's place. It was a bigger house than hers with traces of white paint on it, a large red barn with a pickup truck outside and a red tractor just visible through the open barn doors.

She stopped her truck and turned it off. "Those vehicles will be yours, too, since you're the only heir."

"Didn't expect that. This sure must be God's work. My bus is junk."

"Maybe it's God's work, maybe not." She pushed open her door. "Your Uncle Luke sold off his animals before he died. I can give you a few chickens."

"No need. Never cared for chickens. Wonder if there's anything to eat in the house? I've had but one single doughnut all day."

She got out of the truck and went inside with him. The air was stale and hot, so she opened windows, and a faint breath of air drifted through. She discovered the refrigerator had been cleaned out except for four bottles of Old Original pale ale. The pantry, though, held some canned chili and a box of soda crackers.

"This do you?" she asked, showing him a can of Hormel.

"Make two cans and eat with me. Care for a pale ale?" She nodded, and he went to the refrigerator and opened two.

She watched him as he ate. He'd learned some manners, probably from being a preacher. He didn't lean over and shovel in the food like Hickory, her hired man. Hickory, who'd worked the farm most of his life, lived in a room above the garage. He rarely spoke, and his flat, angular face looked cut from tin. She didn't consider him company-- more like a dependable horse.

Harry poured their beer into glasses instead of drinking from the bottle. She could tell he was more worldly than she was, but she also knew she'd seen things he hadn't.

"I'd like to know what you grow in that herb garden of yours. Looks like you hire a professional gardener."

"I'm the professional gardener."

"Must keep you busy."

"Every day from early spring to near winter. You have to keep at it since there's always varmints destroying plants. Right now, it's the slugs. I hate those things, but I melt them into puddles with table salt."

He laughed. "Never heard of that."

"Beer works, too, but it just drowns them."

"Not a bad way to go," he said, taking a swig of ale.

They both heard a car pull up outside, a door slam, followed by a hard knock on the door. She finished her last spoonful of chili and got up to answer. It was a police officer from Gulch City.

"Hello, Bailey," she said. "What can I help you with?"

He seemed surprised to see her. "It's him I'm looking for," pointing to Harry, who stood and faced him calmly. "Is that your VW bus sitting locked up near the Methodist Church?"

"It is, officer. I had to leave it because the battery's dead. I plan to move it out of there right away."

"Not really the problem. The state police come by a little while ago looking for a man name of Brother Merlin Osgood who goes about in a bus just like that, passing himself off as a traveling evangelist. He's been selling illegal drugs over a four-state area."

"I don't know any person by that name, officer, but that is certainly my bus—registered to me, Reverend Harold Hill, now owner of this farm. My papers are locked inside in the glove box."

"You better come along with me while we check things out, Mr. Hill."

"Call me Harry, since this is my home town."

Dorothy took a step toward Harry. "He's who he says he is, Bailey. I knew him in high school. I'll drive him there and follow behind you. I have jumper cables in my truck. Want a beer before we go?"

Bailey shook his head but seemed to relax. "I'm on duty. Maybe another time. I'll need to search him, just in case." He patted Harry down but never checked his cowboy boots. She watched Harry's smile tighten, then finally loosen when Bailey said, "He's okay," and turned toward the door.

As she followed the police car into Gulch City, Harry pointed to landmarks he remembered, including the Gulch City Bank where he once had a summer job polishing the marble floors. She glanced at the gray stone building, and it was then he slipped the cloth bag out of his boot and underneath the seat.

"That was a long time ago." she said.

The local police, three of them, had a warrant and pulled apart the inside of Harry's van, checking every nook and cranny, floormat, suitcase, guitar sound hole, and pants pocket. They scraped out the ashtrays with a jackknife and tested what they found. They checked the outside under fenders and in the motor. Dorothy sat in her truck watching. Harry leaned patiently on the front of the bus. When they were finally satisfied Harry wasn't Brother Merlin Osgood, Bailey apologized for the trouble and said he was free to go.

"No trouble, officer," Harry said genially. "I know you're just doing your job."

Dorothy pulled her truck up behind his bus, hooked up jumper cables, and had the engine going in about a minute.

Harry started on up the road with extreme caution, and Dorothy followed him impatiently all the way to his place. He pulled the bus up inside the red barn and out of sight. She was sitting on the porch steps waiting for him.

"Glad you came back here," he said, smiling warmly.

"I thought you might want whatever you stuck underneath my seat."

Harry's smile turned sheepish. "You're a crafty one."

"Go and get it, and then we can drink that last beer—and talk a little."

"I intended all the time to tell you about it, maybe even make it a present for all your kindness."

"Did you now?" she said doubtfully. "Are you Brother Merlin Osgood?"

He considered that for only a moment. "At present, I'm Harry Hill."

She laughed hard, stood up, and went inside. Harry got the bag from the truck and went in, feeling a little uncertain of her.

"You aren't the only humbug I ever met." She now stood at the refrigerator, clearly enjoying herself.

She ran all her fingers through her auburn hair, pushing it back behind her ears. Something about the movement opened his eyes. He saw for the first time that, though worn at the edges, she was surprisingly pleasant to look at.

"Were you ever a preacher at all?"

"I was and am. I have a divinity degree glued in my Bible."

"Let's have this beer. I'd be fascinated to hear just what it was got you tossed from the church."

He stood at the table and took a long drink of the beer she gave him. "It's a tale I'm not sure you'll believe."

"You lie some to the police, but I'm willing to listen."

He was a little hurt by the remark but overcame it. "Let's take a seat." She did, and he opened the blue bag and poured the contents on the table. "Know what these are?"

"A bunch of dried mushrooms. What about them?"

"Not just dried mushrooms, *magic* mushrooms."

She laughed. "Like Jack and his magic beans."

"Better than that. You want to hear this or make jokes?"

"I want to hear."

He took a minute to settle. "Well, okay, it all started when this old friend from California came by my parsonage one day trying to sell me these little dried-up fungi. He said that, prepared in the proper way, they'd expand my spiritual being. I told him my spiritual being was just fine, but he kept at me, saying I had nothing to lose and everything to gain. He promised to stay with me the whole time and be a guide. I've never been one to pass up interesting experiences, so he boiled bits of mushrooms into a tea; I drank it down…and in maybe half an hour I took off like a rocket on a trip that blew my head apart and changed my whole way of thinking. I visited another world, Dorothy—the real one, not this gritty old black and white one."

Her face lost all sense of being amused or disbelieving. She took a drink of beer and leaned toward him. "Is this the truth? Was this world in technicolor?"

"It was."

"Keep on going."

So he told her the tale, a fantastic one—of tracking a huge lion, maybe Aslan himself, on a journey up a road paved in gold to a city of flowers and jeweled towers. In the center of the city, he came to a tall, shining tree; the lion turned into a man all in white, glowing like a star, standing in front of the tree with arms outstretched.

The shining man said, "Welcome, Harry Hill—welcome to the fullness of life."

"It surely was God Himself," Harry said in a rising voice. "At that moment I felt I was in an all-encompassing circle of love. I knew without a doubt that evil stood no chance against such power. I saw there was structure and meaning to the world, and I was a part of it. My seminary training was out the window. I understood that God wanted all of us to be saved, not just a select few. Heaven wasn't perfection but a place to go on working towards it. That vision changed me forever."

She was awestruck. "My God, Harry."

"On the very next Sunday, I preached about what I'd seen, my most inspired sermon ever, and they fired me before the week was out."

"Naturally they fired you—no one believed me, either. I walked on a golden road once," she said passionately. "I saw a lion, too, and a shining city. And there were evil people around, but they never won out. I've been to a place like that, Harry."

"I guessed it. There's that faraway look in your eyes."

She sat quiet for a minute, excited but uncertain, thinking of all she wanted to say but doubting that she should. Finally, she took the leap. "When I was twelve, still a young girl, there was this terrible storm, a cyclone, and a tree blew down on the house--went right through the roof and hit me. They say I lay three days in a coma. But when I came out of it, I told a story of a strange, magical place I'd been to and what I'd seen, and no one believed a word. They humored me, of course, because I was a kid. They said it was a dream that people in comas were known to have. In time, I just shut up about it. I wanted more than anything to go back there. But here's the funny thing: when I was there, I wanted in the worst way to be home. And when I was home again, I wanted to go back. I guess I didn't know what I wanted. Both places, I think. But that's not possible."

Harry smiled wisely. "You sure of that?"

The following suppertime Harry spent at Dorothy's house. Hickory took his food in his room above the garage, saying he wasn't feeling well. Harry and Dorothy were glad to be left alone.

"It's his heart," she said. "He's had some trouble."

They ate a light meal of chicken soup and cornbread. Afterwards, Harry ground up a dried mushroom in her coffee grinder. He measured out a teaspoon of the powder and mixed it in a glass of lemonade.

"You'll stay with me for sure?" she asked.

"I won't move from your side. That's a promise."

She sat down on her own familiar couch, drank the lemonade, and stretched out with a pillow underneath her head. Harry pulled a chair up beside her, covered her eyes with a folded hand towel, and began playing old hymns softly on his acoustic guitar. She sighed, and the sound of it was pleasure to him. She clicked her heels together to the rhythm of the music. As he played, he wondered if there might be a small hidden place in her garden to grow some new things. Though he now owned a farm, he was no farmer, but wondered if some church in town might be open to a musician with a new brand of music, or the high school a band director with a youthful, innovative sound? He'd begun to feel half at home in this place.

As the guitar music grew softer, Dorothy stepped out onto a golden road under giant rainbows arching the sky and white blossoms falling about her like snow. Ahead was a field of ruby-colored flowers. She was full of joyful wonderment. Could she really live in two worlds at once, with a traveling companion who knew the way? For the first time ever, it seemed halfway feasible.

STAR BAKER

To Adrian's utter disbelief, Meera Das lost in the semi-finals of the Great British Baking Show because of that surly bastard Paul Hollywood, who criticized her Show-Stopper four-layer honey sponge cake, claiming the sponge was slightly over baked and dry from too little honey. Adrian had seen her test each layer of sponge with a knife, and she was satisfied. Prue, the other judge, loved the flavor and design, but of the final four contestants (after nine grueling weeks of competition), Meera was the one eliminated. It made no sense. Just the previous week she'd been chosen Star Baker. Adrian sat rigid with shock—Meera was so exceptional.

There with his mother in the tiny parlor of their Birmingham flat, he pounded a knee with his fist.

"Paul Hollywood has something against her," he choked out. His mother, whose flowered housedress seemed to disappear into the fading roses of the wallpaper, nodded, watching the other contestants hug and console Meera, an alluring, olive-skinned girl in her mid-twenties—dark glossy hair, huge brown eyes. Adrian took out a large handkerchief and wiped his eyes and nose. He couldn't control his emotions, so he quickly rose from the sagging recliner and left the room.

"She's a lovely one," his mother called after him. "I'll miss her, Adrian. Such a nice personality. And so humble about her abilities. I loved the way she helped the others when things went wrong."

Adrian was too emotional to answer. He was suffering. Over the many weeks of the competition, he had felt his heart slowly fill with her gracious spirit until now it was close to bursting. Thanks to Paul Hollywood, though, he would probably never see her again.

The next day was Saturday, but he was a letter carrier and had to work. The job was tedious, yet it afforded him many solitary hours to stew and ruminate and plan. He had learned from the show that Meera had been born in London, raised there by immigrant parents from Delhi. She lived and worked as a baker in Southall, the east part of London. Nothing had been mentioned of any serious relationship in her life.

He wasn't delusional enough to make that his goal. All he hoped to do was in some way offer her solace. Vengeful thoughts kept interfering with his better nature. He had nothing against Prue, who was firm but fair in her decisions. Noel and Matt, the gadflies, were clowns who disrupted the concentration of contestants. They were sometimes funny, often irritating, but he bore them no grudge. It was Paul Hollywood who deserved to be punished, and before Adrian's route was done, he had thought of several imaginative (if excessive) ways to accomplish it. Midway through the block on Kelsey Street, a dog came lunging after him, and he raised his can of pepper spray, dispatching the beast with a short blast.

By the time Adrian arrived back at the flat for dinner, a sketchy plan was beginning to form.

"Might take a few days off," he told his mother, who was pulling two meat pies out of the oven. "There's vacation time I haven't used. I may lose it if I don't do something soon."

"That's a good idea. Where will you go?"

"London, maybe. Not far. I don't know yet. Just need a breather from Birmingham and the job."

"Be sure to be back for the baking show, son. The finals are next Friday. I'm on pins and needles."

He went to the fridge and lifted a bottle of Guinness. "I don't know…I'm losing my feel for it now that Meera's out. Damn that Paul Hollywood."

"Oh, he can be grumpy at times, but I like him. He's very good looking and just my age."

Adrian snorted out a laugh. "You and Paul Hollywood. There's a pair. He'd tell you your meat pies are wonky and over baked. You're dreaming, mum. He's not a nice man."

"Oh, well, look who's talking about dreaming? You've been silly over that Meera for weeks now. You think I don't know my own son? If you like her that much, go see her. What's to lose? You're single and only a few years older than her. She just works in Southall—two hours down the road."

"You're the silly one. TV and reality are two different things. I know the difference."

She grinned at him. "*Do* you now?" She used a spatula to lift the meat pies onto plates, and went on grinning. She could read him like one of her tabloids.

Adrian drove the M-40 toward Berkshire, site of Welford Park Estate where Love Productions filmed the show. If that didn't turn up what he wanted, it was east to Canterbury (home of Paul Hollywood) by way of the M-25. He'd be in the Queen's Arms bed and breakfast, Uxbridge, by nightfall, then off the following morning to Southall to find the bakery where Meera Das did her star baking.

His aging Mini Cooper was smoking a bit, burning oil, but he'd never known it to quit on him. He passed out of the haze of Birmingham and into the countryside, and his heart began to sail like those landfill gulls he could see riding the winds above him. He was embarking on a quest, dedicated to a fair lady, the fairest he'd seen. Though she didn't know he existed, she would be aware of him very soon, and that knowledge would be reward enough—for him, at least. Dizzying, he thought—this tidal wave of feeling. Something life-changing was happening inside. His existence now possessed a focus and a glow—the patina of old bronze. Her remembered voice (as she described her cake ingredients) was like music to him, like a sweet melody, like Sting's "Fields of Gold."

Being a mail carrier made him glad in ways: the exercise left him strong and lean and not really all that bad to look at even if his hairline was receding. He played football on the weekends. He could dance some…the girls usually said yes when he asked. He had a decent job, though nothing to go on about. He knew how middle of the road he really was, yet he also knew his heart was larger than most. He could feel it growing daily, its space for love swelling like one of those yeasty breads she baked. Truth is, she wasn't a tv star—just a baker, as common as himself.

At Berkshire, the Welford Park Estate was locked up tight and deserted-looking—obviously no production going on at present. Through the gate he could see the huge baking tent where she had labored so many weeks. The additional two-and-a-half-hour trip to Canterbury now became a necessity, but he felt strangely elated about facing difficulties…no true quest should ever be simple.

He skirted London to the south and soon found the scenery as agreeable as his mood—a road through Surrey Hills with woodlands, hillsides purple with heather, rolling fields etched by streams, and ponds dazzling in sunlight. Small country villages appeared magically, like Brigadoon, as if from centuries before. He passed through market towns with names like Hog's Back and Box Hill—a part of his own island country of England he'd never before seen. How narrow he'd allowed his life to be, how limited and provincial! How wide the door she'd thrown open for him!

Paul's house was not difficult to find. The internet posted dozens of photos of it inside and out and pinpointed the location. He'd studied the stories on Paul, read that the large country house dated from the Middle Ages. He parked down the narrow road from it and turned off the engine. He had a clear view of the driveway and garage. As he waited, he opened a bag and nibbled on one of his mother's Manchester tarts. The raspberry jam inside was commercial, the pastry cloyingly sweet—not at all the work of a Star Baker.

An hour passed slowly, and he began to worry about flaws in his plan. But then the garage door opened suddenly, jarring him awake, and a black Mercedes sedan swung inside. The garage door churned down again. A moment later, Paul Hollywood emerged from a side door, followed, to Adrian's astonishment, by Prue herself. She had on her red glasses. The two went briskly into the house.

How strange seeing them, the real flesh and blood, not the tv images. If he was truthful, though, they seemed as familiar to him as the neighbors in his own block of flats. He'd been regularly socializing with baking show celebrities for quite some time.

He sat still as stone, beset by ongoing doubts. What was Prue doing here? Was it right that she be party to this when his business was with Paul only? Yet he'd come this far. To leave without completing the task would be unthinkable, a waste. He eased out of the door of his Mini, crept to the rear and opened the boot, lifting out a gallon glass jug. Paul had left the side door to the garage unlocked. A security camera on the house pointed away from the area. Perfect. In the blink of an eye, he was inside and on about his business.

There were more bakeries in Southall than he'd ever imagined, but by eleven the next morning, he sat parked in front of The Royal Bakery with a broad smile on his face. A large canvas sign draped across the front window broadcast her presence: STAR BAKER MEERA DAS WORKS HER MAGIC HERE!

He'd found her. His own tenacity and surprising competence excited him. How lost those character qualities were on a mail-carrying job. He'd been lazy in his life, he knew all too well; he'd willingly settled for less. For her sake, though, he would rise in the world.

He entered The Royal Bakery carrying an array of carnations wrapped in pink tissue paper. A heavyset bald man in a white tee shirt and apron with black burn marks eyed him suspiciously.

"Let me guess," he said. "You're here with flowers for Meera."

"Well, yes, but I'd like some of her baked goods, too."

"She's not here at present, sorry to say. But the Battenburg cakes are hers. The Empire biscuits, too."

"Four Empire biscuits," Adrian said. "And see that she gets these," handing over the flowers. "I'm an old friend. Tell her that. I just want to consol her on her loss. It was an injustice, as far as I'm concerned."

The bald man grinned, showing gnarly teeth. "Don't know it's a loss. She's doubled our business. She's signed a contract to write a cookbook. She made Star Baker once, you know."

"Oh, I know. She's amazing."

He used oil paper to lift the Empire biscuits into a bag. "Funny, we get blokes coming in with flowers almost every day—some of them wanting to marry her, even. It's more notoriety than she wants, I have to say. She's a private, simple girl."

"I'm just an old friend," Adrian said, paying for the biscuits. As he turned toward the door, he caught just a glimpse of Meera carrying a bowl across the kitchen.

He returned to The Royal Bakery with flowers (daisies with one large sunflower) at ten the next morning. The same man, clearly the owner, came over to greet him. "You're a persistent one," he said.

"I caught a glimpse of her yesterday."

"We have to protect her, you understand."

"Of course I understand. Give me a few slices of her Battenburg today and tell her the same old friend stopped."

"Baking show fans aren't all the same, see. Some can be weird, and some downright cruel. Especially the ones on social media. You seem nice enough, but we have to be careful. I'll give her the flowers and let her know you came by again."

On the third morning, Adrian carried roses and purchased her Manchester tarts to compare to his mother's. When once again she wouldn't come out, he went to his car that he'd parked directly across the street. The raspberry jam was so delectable, the pastry so buttery and subtle that he closed his eyes and told himself he'd wait all day, all evening, if necessary, for her to emerge.

Near noon, as he half dozed, he heard a tapping at the window. He was startled to see Meera Das standing beside his car, her huge brown eyes peering in. He quickly turned down the window. He saw that those beautiful eyes were guarded, apprehensive, and he understood why.

"You're not an old friend," she said, with a curtness he'd never heard in her voice. "Why are you saying that?"

"I'm sorry," he replied with honest remorse. "I swear I'm not stalking you. I just loved you on the show. You were marvelous. I wanted to say I was so sorry you lost. I wanted to console you. I felt Paul Hollywood was very unfair—a monster, in fact. You didn't deserve it."

She stared as if weighing his words. Then she seemed to soften a little. "There's a tea shop down the street. Could we talk there a few minutes?"

"I'd like that. Care for something to eat?"

"No…just a cup of tea—please."

They sat down in the quaint Indian teashop in a booth with a soft curved sofa seat that brought them closer together than separate chairs. The place was hung with ferns, the tables set with fresh sprigs of lilac. He noticed a bust of Queen Victoria, a carved elephant, and several small statues he guessed were Hindu gods and goddesses. He hadn't factored her cultural differences into his sense of her, but they didn't matter. She seemed English through and through even if she wasn't.

She ordered ginger chai, and he asked for Earl Grey from a pretty Indian woman in a purple and green sari. She knew Meera and was friendly toward them. She brought their tea, went away, and Meera began to talk.

"You're very wrong about Paul Hollywood. His gruffness is just an act for the show. He's extremely nice off camera--a kind, funny man. He was right about my honey sponge cake. I measured the honey in the wrong proportion. The others who won did better. They deserved what they got. To tell the truth, I'm almost glad I didn't win. The winners have suffered because of people who think I was cheated. Some have sent very ugly messages online. It's sad what some fans do. Just plain cruel. It ruins everything good that happened to us."

"I...I'm sorry. I didn't realize..." He'd intended to hint at his role in redressing her grievance—but recognized a sure path to disaster.

"A few even act out their aggressions. Actually do malicious acts. Can you imagine it? Because of a tv baking show?"

"What do you mean?"

"Well, just for example—a few nights ago, someone poured honey all over Prue's car while she was visiting Paul. Even squirted honey in the door locks. It caused quite a lot of damage. The police are looking for whoever did it."

"Prue's car? Are you sure?" He was horrified. "That's terrible. I'd think it would be Paul's car."

A frown creased her smooth olive forehead. "Why would you say that?"

He felt momentary panic yet managed to calm himself and right the ship. "Well...isn't it obvious? Prue is so nice, and Paul is...or seems...so stern and cold. And then the connection to your honey cake—not enough honey, he said...must be someone meaning to right the wrong done to you."

Her frown evaporated. "Of course. That's brilliant! I hadn't thought of it! The honey cake!"

He relaxed a little then, and so did she. It seemed he'd managed to save the day. Brilliant was her word. Indeed.

"Of course, it's clear enough now—the honey cake," she repeated, nodding. Something measurable changed in her attitude; she warmed to him, and he saw again the gracious spirit he'd so admired on the show. She was much too trusting to suspect him of malicious behavior. He'd mistakenly done a terrible wrong to Prue, whom he admired. He felt remorse, but quickly forgave himself knowing she could afford a fleet of such cars.

He blew on his tea as she sipped her chai. She looked up at him and smiled. "I liked your flowers," she said. "But please don't ask me to marry you."

"Hadn't thought of it," he replied with a laugh. "I hear you've had offers."

She nodded, blushing a little. "Are you from London?"

"Birmingham. Just down for a short holiday. Have to get back today. The final bake is tonight, you know. I watch the show just for fun. My mum is hooked on it."

"We filmed a few months ago, so I know who wins—but I can't tell you. I'm sworn to secrecy."

"Should've been you that won, no matter what you say. You're Star Baker in my eyes."

"You're sweet…umm, did you tell me your name?"

"I didn't. It's Adrian. Adrian Hyde."

"What is your line of work, then?"

"A mail carrier right now. I have bigger plans, though."

"That's an important job."

Something began to glow inside him. He understood why she had offers of marriage. She was as perfect as female creation got.

"Would you mind sharing your cell number so I could text you some time?" she asked. "You very much overdid it with the flowers— they worried me. But you're different than I thought. You seem like a very nice person."

His cell was in the car, so he wrote down his number on a napkin. She gave him hers in return. He folded her napkin like a sacred object and tucked it carefully into his shirt pocket. Through the front window he noticed a red Aston Martin pull to the front of the bakery. She stood abruptly.

"That's Paul Hollywood. I've got to go."

"Paul Hollywood is picking you up?"

"It's not what you think. He's taking me to meet a publisher. Just business."

She bent and kissed him on the cheek. "It's been lovely meeting you, Adrian. Thank you." She went out of the tearoom, glancing back at him once with a smile, then crossing just behind his Mini Cooper, pausing a moment, and then jumping into the Aston Martin. Still thunderstruck by the kiss, he sat staring as the Aston Martin roared away. His mother was never going to believe this. He felt like Star Baker and Arthur of Camelot wrapped into one.

That night, as his mother and he watched The Great British Baking Show closing competition, eating fish and chips at their tv tables, he realized he felt connected to these people as never before. His mum *had* believed him when he told her he'd met Meera Das and gotten her cell number and a kiss, that he'd actually seen Paul Hollywood in his Aston Martin going off with Meera to a publisher. His mum had always recognized his potential, even if he'd rarely risen to it. But now he stood on the brink of confirming her faith.

Bella, the Italian grandmother, did best in the Signature Bake with her Bomboloni. Hans the Hollander appeared to win the Technical Bake with his Appelflap. As the Showstopper Bake was about to be judged, they heard a sharp knock at the door. Adrian ignored it at first, but it persisted.

"Mum, would you go? I don't want to miss the end."

"It's never for me. It'll be one of your pals."

"Damn, what a time!"

"I'll tell you what happens, son."

"That's just perfect, miss the final champion," he snapped at her, pushing himself angrily to his feet. As he passed through the kitchen to the door, he heard the text tone sounding on his phone. He lifted the cell and read the screen: "Adrian. Prue will drop charges if you pay the damages of £1432. I'd advise it. Might save your job." Staggered, he steadied himself against a countertop and pulled the folded napkin from his pocket. It wasn't the same number—of course not—as if she'd give it out at all. He found himself struggling to breathe.

The knocking went on, and finally he tossed open the door. Two constables in white shirts, black ties, stab vests and reflective jackets stood frowning at him.

"Adrian Hyde?" the older of the two asked. "We'd like a look in the boot of your Mini. Here's a warrant."

"Seems to be crawling with ants," the other one added, stroking his thick moustache, amused. "Not the sharpest tack in the box, are ye, son?"

FATHER'S GIRL

Amber Lowell's mother Jackie, with whom she'd had an uneasy relationship, died in early September at the age of forty-seven within eight months of her pancreatic cancer diagnosis. Mark, Amber's older brother and only sibling, was in law school on the East Coast. Though distraught (he had been close to their mother) he had returned to school two days after the funeral. Her father, weary from care-giving, shaken by the loss, still took only a week off teaching and then went back. He found writing impossible, yet he needed to be doing something. Fall semester at the university involved only three graduate classes, which he insisted he could manage.

Ezra Lowell, PhD. was an attractive, charming man. At forty-eight, he had four modestly successful novels to his credit, and a full professorship. Amber adored him and felt they'd always had a special relationship. She read books he recommended, and they often talked about them—intelligently, she felt, though she was younger and less educated than his students. He read her fledgling attempts at writing and gave her encouragement. It took little for her to make the decision to put off starting college for a year and stay home to see to her father while they both worked at revising their lives.

He was apprehensive about it yet knew that Amber, now nineteen, was nearly as good at running a house as her mother had been. Their house was a large, aging brick Tudor near the university; it took work. Her mother had expected a great deal of her, far more than of Mark, her golden boy. Though Amber felt pain about the loss of her mother, in some ways it was a relief to have her gone.

On top of the domestic responsibilities, including cooking, Amber offered to take over the secretarial work her mother had done—typing his handwritten manuscripts into the computer, sorting through his multiple emails, paying bills. That brought a light to his eyes. He considered her offer for less than a day before agreeing to it. It lifted a weight off him, and she felt mature and valued. She had no idea there would be others vying for space in his life.

They started arriving not long after the funeral. Bea Davis had been a friend of her mother from college. She lived on a lake an hour north, a vacation home she'd gained in a divorce. In spite of too much makeup, she was a glamorous, full-figured woman. She arrived one late morning without even a phone call first.

"Hello, Amber," she said breezily. "I have something for your father and you." She carried a bottle of wine in a bag and something in a foil pan, brushed past Amber who hadn't asked her in, and went straight to the kitchen, depositing her packages on the counter beside the sink.

"It's my chicken parmesan. You'll have to heat it up. Instructions are taped to the top. There's a bottle of pinot grigio in the bag. Where is Ezra?"

"Upstairs in his office."

"I'll go say hello for a minute."

"Umm, he doesn't like to be disturbed while he's working."

"Oh, he'll want to see me, dear." And off she went.

Amber found a spot for the foil pan in the refrigerator and glanced at the pot roast she had ready to go for tonight's dinner. She sighed and decided it could wait a day. Within twenty minutes Bea Davis descended the creaky staircase and came back into the kitchen smiling. "He loves chicken parmesan. He says you're taking very good care of him, Amber…a real comfort—quite a father's girl. I'd love to buy you lunch sometime soon. Would you have any time?"

"Lunch with me?" she asked, surprised.

"Your Mom was a friend. I think we both need to talk about her."

"Well…sure, I guess."

"I'd like to be friends with you, too."

Amber glanced at the floor. "Okay…" a bit tentatively.

"I won't rush this. Maybe in a few weeks?"

Amber nodded and watched Bea Davis find her way to the door.

Her father nearly always had two graduate assistants working in his office and doing research for him. This year both were females, attractive in very different ways. One, Nell O'Day, known to be something of a poet, sported a small red rosebud tattoo on her neck matched by a slash of bright red lipstick; she dressed in black thrift store clothing, and as far as Amber could tell, never wore a bra. Amber wished she dared be more like her.

The other was brainy and seductive. Her name was Clarissa Walters, and her body was lush in ways Amber's never would be. If her father judged women by looks, Amber could never compete with Clarissa. Nor could she match her in wit or intellect. Clarissa had it all and knew it. When she began showing up several times a week with work she'd done for him, disappearing for long periods into her father's office, Amber grew uneasy, vaguely sensing a threat.

Within several weeks Bea, as promised, asked her to lunch at Leo's, an expensive seafood place downtown on the river. Bea was perfumed and dressed in a tight black skirt and a yellow cashmere sweater against which her breasts strained. Except for bursts of wrinkles around her eyes, she looked alluring. Amber, in slacks and a plain white blouse, felt like a file clerk. Bea ordered a glass of sauvignon blanc and Amber a Coke.

"I'd suggest the seafood linguini," Bea said. "The wine sauce is amazing."

Amber nodded her approval and pushed aside the leather-bound menu.

Bea opened her purse and removed a small, gift-wrapped box. "I have a present for you, dear."

"A present? Why?"

"Just to lift your spirits. Open it."

Puzzled, Amber carefully unwrapped it to find a box marked Swarovski. Inside was a designer pen.

"Ezra tells me you're thinking of following in his footsteps as a writer."

"I really don't know. But, thanks, this is lovely." She looked at Bea, whose eyes gleamed with good will.

They ordered, chatted about Bea's son, who was Mark's age and in the military. Amber sipped her Coke, wishing she were old enough for a glass of wine. It seemed plain that Bea was courting her to curry favor with her father.

As if on cue, Bea turned the subject to Ezra. "Your father is such a talent, such a fascinating man. If Jackie hadn't been a friend, I might have been tempted." She laughed a bit too loudly at this. "Your father is so warm, so outgoing, and Jackie seemed…well…more and more insular as the years went by. I suspect Ezra's light got too bright for her. It can happen, you know. She was a background person. Fortunately, Ezra had a loving daughter for emotional support. Let me give you some advice, though, dear. Don't try to be a replacement for your mother. It never works."

"I'm nothing like my mother, Bea."

'Of course you aren't, Amber, and I know you'll be smart about this."

Six weeks after the funeral, Ezra began writing again, and he soon handed over his barely decipherable longhand pages to Amber. When she was small, he would enthrall her with tales at bedtime, stories like *The Wendigo* or ones of his own making, which scared her to sleep. Now he was weaving tales again—for her to transform into print. Invited into his life as never before, she was sharing a first look at what he was creating. She wondered what, if anything, her mother had felt about the experience.

His writing process was far more labor-intensive than she'd ever imagined. Sometimes he'd rework a line dozens of times; then when he read what she'd typed, he'd often start over. He seemed to love doing it. "If you push and pull at words, graceful accidents happen," he told her. "It's a magic I can't explain. If you get serious about writing, you'll find out."

During this period, she felt closer to him than ever before—closer, it seemed to her, than her mother had been, though the relationship of her parents remained a mystery to her. During Amber's teenage years her parents had seemed to grow more separate; they shared daily life, but like business partners. They rarely argued, except about her mother's sharp demands on her, her father feeling they were often unjust. He usually took Amber's side, and her mother would back off resentfully and go off by herself. Her silence would weigh heavy in the house for a day or more and then gradually dissipate like a storm cloud.

The English Department of the university was on the side of campus nearest the shopping district. Amber enjoyed the mellow autumn days, the dignified houses and ancient golden trees as she walked her father to classes, continuing on to shop for groceries. Along the way they passed fraternity and sorority houses hung with Greek letters, flags, football banners. Students passed by and often spoke warmly to Ezra. He was a beloved teacher, she knew, and female students seemed awed by him. Being his daughter was not a hardship. Most of her friends were away at college, yet her father more than filled that empty space; she lived happily in his glow.

Their house was set on a huge double lot with several dozen mature maples and oaks. Leaves fell nonstop through late October into December. Her father sometimes hired a lawn service to do the work, but this year Nell O'Day, who seemed always short of money, asked him for the job. He reluctantly agreed, yet in no time realized she went at the work with passionate energy, using a backpack blower to send great clouds of leaves spinning into the woods behind the house. She wore torn jeans, a pea coat, a black knit cap, and men's work boots. Amber watched her with admiration. The elfin creature seemed to bring light and grace to everything she did. Amber longed to know her better.

Ezra began going out to dinner, a movie, or a football game with Bea every week or two. She also overheard him in his office reading aloud to Clarissa Walters, often until quite late at night. As Clarissa was going out the door one Friday near midnight, Amber stopped her and asked, "What is my father reading to you?"

She smiled coyly while zipping up her red leather coat and flipping her blonde hair over the collar. "He wants my opinion of his latest chapters. I seem to be a help to him. I assume he does the same with you."

"Sometimes," Amber muttered. The truth was, he never asked her opinion of his writing. She was his typist.

Amber noticed a trace of lipstick on one of Clarissa's perfect front teeth, like a spot of blood in a cat's mouth. She wondered for a moment how wise a man her father really was.

The next morning Amber made him a breakfast of French toast and bacon, one of his favorites. As she sipped her coffee and watched him eat and then pack his briefcase, she asked, "Are you really reading drafts to Clarissa? She said you were."

"Yes. Do you mind?"

"A little, I guess. I thought I might be the one."

He smiled, reached across the table and patted her hand. "You will be one day. Clarissa is working on a doctorate, honey. She has an amazing and perceptive creative mind. I can see her as a top editor in a few years. You aren't at that level yet. But you help me in a hundred other ways. You're my right-hand girl. I couldn't do without you."

His encouragement disheartened her.

Two nights later she heard Clarissa, her father's dedicated first responder, slip out of the house after 3 a.m. Through her bedroom window she saw her roll her VW Beetle into the street before starting it.

On an evening soon after, Ezra took Bea to dinner and then to the ballet. When they got home after midnight, it had begun to snow heavily. Amber watched the huge flakes fall through the gleam of a streetlight. It reminded her of her childhood, of Christmas, and she thought of her mother decorating the house and singing along with carols on the radio. There had been happiness once a long time ago. Whatever had happened after that was a mystery to her.

In the morning, as Amber headed toward the bathroom, she met Bea Davis coming out of it, hair wrapped in a towel and wearing Ezra's robe. Bea smiled, not the least embarrassed, offering no explanation. "Hello, Amber," she chirped. "The bathroom is all yours," and meandered back into her father's bedroom. Amber locked the bathroom door and stood under the shower in a daze.

Bea stayed for breakfast, described for Amber the high points of last night's ballet, expressed relief that the roads had been cleared, and kissed Ezra's cheek. He rose and saw her out to her car. He returned in a moment, sat across from Amber, and refilled his coffee cup.

"She was supposed to be gone before you got up," he said quietly.

"She slept with you."

"Yeah, what a surprise. I'm human."

Amber stared into the reflection of a window on the surface of her coffee. "Please don't jump into another relationship, Dad. It's way too soon." Her concern, she knew, was mostly jealous resentment.

He laughed. "Oh, honey, I have no intention of jumping into anything—with anyone. Bea may have other ideas, but I don't."

"What about Clarissa?"

She seemed to hit a nerve. "What about her?"

"I know it isn't any of my business…"

"It certainly is *not* any of your business." He paused, drank some coffee, and gathered himself. "I've been thinking, Amber. You've put off college for my sake—for which I'm genuinely thankful—but I know I've been selfish. I think you should get on down the road to Ann Arbor and start school in January."

She was stunned. "Who will do what I'm doing?"

He shrugged and looked out the window. "I'm sure I'll figure out something. I don't want you putting your life on hold for me."

There was little doubt about it: her presence was cramping his style.

Amber's domestic life began to seem less fulfilling. She was quiet with her father for several days, but he refused to be anything but pleasant, so she warmed to him again. In the back of her mind, though, was the perception that he was savoring life and she was missing something. They didn't speak again of her starting college in January, so she did nothing to make it happen. She remained his right-hand girl, and some days that was enough.

Several weeks before Christmas, when she'd decorated the tree and Nell had put up the wreaths and outside lights, Ezra cautiously asked Amber if she would mind sorting through her mother's clothing and doing something with it—getting it off it to Goodwill or the Salvation Army. Nell happened to overhear this and volunteered to help. Amber agreed to do it for no other reason than to be in Nell's company. In truth, she dreaded the job, though it had to be done. Nell asked to be paid only in things she might be able to use for herself. There was nothing Amber would possibly consider keeping. The thought of Nell wearing something of her mother's was too strange to think about.

Ezra insisted on being gone when they did it. Her mother's clothing was located in a large, walk-in closet next to one of the guest bedrooms. Jackie Lowell—small, attractive, fastidious—had kept her clothing perfectly folded in drawers, color-coding her hanging rows of dresses, blouses, and sweaters. Nell looked through them with high interest, as if shopping.

"Your mother was certainly neat," she said, lifting down a long black dress.

"Obsessive, maybe?"

Nell nodded and held the dress against her. "Mind if I try it?"

"You can have whatever you want."

To her surprise Nell stripped off her sweater and jeans.

Except for wool socks and black panties, she was naked. Her small, firm breasts were pink-tipped, her skin smooth and milky, her hips softly curved. She was delicate, sylphlike. Amber was amazed and looked away as Nell pulled the dress over her head.

"Damn—not quite my size. Maybe the skirts and blouses will work." She set aside the dress and went searching for more. Amber watched as she got in and out of clothes, not the least self-conscious about her nakedness. Amber had seen naked girls before in locker rooms, but this one, fully a woman, affected her differently. Nell was so much freer than other women, than Amber herself. She loved her for it. She wanted to absorb whatever it was that Nell had.

Nell found a few blouses and a black pencil skirt that fit. She moved on to the drawers of several large dressers. In a half drawer near the top of one, she found lingerie.

"Look at this stuff. It's still wrapped. It's never been worn. Come on, Amber, you can try these. It's lingerie your mother never even opened. It's gorgeous."

"I just can't, Nell. It's too weird."

"Let's both try it. It turns me on just looking at it."

Amber took a deep breath and came over to see. Knowing any hesitation would stop her, she stripped naked and put on a white teddy as Nell watched. Nell put on black. They looked each other over, nervously admiring what they saw. Nell stepped closer, leaned forward and kissed her. Amber hesitated, pulled away, changed her mind and returned the kiss, touching Nell's breasts with trembling fingers. She was shocked at her turbulent feelings.

Later, when they'd packed everything but a few pieces of lingerie into Nell's rusty Jeep, Nell kissed and thanked her. "I couldn't resist you in that little white outfit."

"I know." Amber smiled warmly, touched the red rosebud on Nell's neck with a fingertip, feeling something like love for this woman.

"I honestly didn't plan this. I really do like men," Nell said.

"Me, too."

"A man like your father, for instance. I just adore him. I think he's gorgeous."

"My father?" her smile fading. "I'm afraid you'll have to get in line."

Nell laughed. "Oh, I can't compete."

"No need to compete. You're great the way you are."

"You're sweet." She kissed Amber again, jumped in the Jeep and drove off.

Amber folded the lingerie Nell hadn't wanted into a pillowcase and carried it to her room (for what reason she wasn't sure). She wondered why her mother had never opened any of the delicate packages. Had they been gifts from Ezra?

It pained her just a bit that this strange, heart-stopping experience with Nell had not, as it turned out, belonged entirely to her. Somehow, her father had, in some inadvertent way, slipped into it.

Just before Christmas break, Nell began appearing at the house to meet with Ezra about a poetry manuscript she was working hard to complete. Nell greeted her with a smile whenever they ran into each other, but Nell's mind was on the poetry and her mentor's thoughts about it. The hours they spent in his office tormented Amber. Why were young women drawn to him like moths to light? Why did she imagine the worst about what transpired behind his closed door?

Her brother Mark arrived on the morning of December 23, planning to stay only a few days. He looked tired and gaunt. He'd inherited some of their father's good looks but not much of his charm. Mark and Amber had never been close. She could remember no heart-to-heart conversations they'd ever had. As a younger sister, she'd longed to connect, but some barrier stood between them. He'd mostly ignored her, confiding only in their mother, and gone his own way, another family mystery. Yet their first day together, with Ezra out at some meeting, Mark opened a bottle of wine, poured them both a glass, and sat down across from her at the kitchen counter. She was grumpily preparing hors d'oeuvres for a last-minute gathering for a former poet in residence who'd shown up unannounced to promote his new book. Ezra, the university's most prominent literary light, commonly hosted such events. His department chair was coming, along with maybe a dozen others.

"How is it going with Ezra?" he asked.

"Okay, I guess." She was washing a colander of shrimp but stopped to take a drink of wine.

"Is he having a tough time without mom?"

"I don't know. His social life seems lively enough."

He went silent, thinking about that. He watched as she prepared the shrimp; also, a casserole dish of meatballs in a spicy sauce, fruit on skewer sticks, wheel of Brie, sliced cheeses and salami with fancy crackers, guacamole dip, deviled eggs on a platter, assorted nuts and mustards, chocolate cookies from France, blueberry cheesecake. He laughed as she labored. "You're doing the same stuff she did."

"Why wouldn't I? She taught me."

"It's amusing to see."

She glanced at him and shook her head. "Why don't you stay through the break, Mark? You're always rushing off."

"I can't help it. It's not you, it's him."

This puzzled her, but she wanted to hear more. "Him?"

"Dad. He's so damned…beloved. His students are like disciples. When he's holding court, I feel myself disappearing into the wood-work."

"It's not that bad."

"We all dance to his agenda. I just got here and instead of resting up after exams, I have to suffer through a party for some damn poet, some self-absorbed phony. I wish I hadn't come."

"He says it'll only last a few hours."

Mark laughed sharply. "Right. He always told mom the same thing." He drank off his wine and poured some more. "Anyway, I may just tell him I'm tired from the trip and stay upstairs."

"You can't ditch me, Mark."

He smiled a little—a rarity. "Oh, all right, little sister."

As it turned out, only ten people showed up because of the holidays, among them Nell O'Day and Clarissa Walters. Nell wore the black pencil skirt and a red silk blouse unbuttoned halfway. Clarissa was only faintly more discreet in a clinging wool dress. The department chair, Lou Thomas, was a white-haired Englishman with bad teeth and a pleasant sense of humor. Three were widowed or unmarried English Department profs, all mildly eccentric older women with no holiday plans. The others were unfamiliar to her.

The poet, whose name was Harry Biggs, showed up last by taxi. Amber dimly remembered him from parties some years before. He was an odd-looking man about her father's age, with a beefy red face— built like a large dwarf, all muscled and gnarly. He'd taught at the university as poet in residence for several years. She remembered him as rather subdued compared to other writers who'd visited them. Most tended to blather non-stop. Harry Biggs was a quiet man who carried a briefcase containing a dozen copies of his new book of poems.

After being greeted like a long-absent family member, he shrugged off his heavy wool overcoat and went to the kitchen to find Amber and Mark, who were opening wine bottles.

"I wanted to tell you how sorry I am about your mother," he said. "She was a lovely woman." He looked at them with his heavy dark eyes, smiled wanly, then pivoted and returned to the gathering before Amber could thank him.

"Remember him?" Mark said in a whisper. "He was at the funeral."

"That was nice of him to say something."

"Yeah. He's a bit of an oddball, but not nearly so full of himself as most of them. Mom liked him, as I recall."

Amber made several trips carrying food to the dining room table; Mark followed with wine bottles. Glasses, silverware, and China plates already lay in place. Several guests poured harder stuff at the massive walnut liquor cabinet. Harry Biggs was one of them. He seemed nervous and in need of a drink. Nell hung near to him, engaging him whenever possible. Amber passed by them once and heard her say, "I write poetry, too, but I've never dared try traditional verse forms like you sometimes do in your books. I never get the sense that you're restricted by the demands of difficult forms."

"Well, I happen to like the restrictions," he answered quietly, glancing down at her cleavage and then away. "I like having my hands tied."

"I don't." And she laughed. "But it doesn't mean I couldn't learn to like it."

The innuendo was too much. Amber went back to the kitchen, disappointed at her friend. Nell hung close to his side like a groupie. Clarissa, in similar fashion, stayed very near Ezra, now and then attaching to his arm. The three older ladies grazed at the food table, the shrimp disappearing almost magically. Amber refilled the bowl twice. Mark helped her open more wine, clear the small China plates smeared with sauces and half-eaten meatballs. She watched the ongoing grinding of teeth and mopping of lips (disgusting, really) and half-listened as Lou Thomas set the stage for Harry to read his poems.

Harry was gradually getting drunk, but he read with surprising clarity. Most of the partygoers seemed attentive and enthusiastic, especially the women.

Amber, half listening but occasionally catching a poignant phrase, noticed Mark staring at Clarissa throughout the event. "She's dad's grad assistant, if you're interested," she whispered.

"Wow. She's amazing. Looks about my age."

"She is. Be my guest."

"I don't compete with Ezra."

By one a.m., Harry Biggs was staggering and inarticulate. Ezra wrestled him into his coat and sat him down in a large chair near the door. "We need to get him back to his hotel," he said to no one in particular.

"I'll take him," Nell volunteered.

"Not you, Nell. Amber, will you do it?"

Understanding, grateful in a way for his caution, she said yes.

She backed Ezra's Volvo out of the garage, and Lou and her father got Harry and his briefcase into the passenger seat. The hotel was only fifteen minutes away, but by the time she arrived at the entrance, he seemed to have sobered a bit. They sat in the entry drive for at least a minute before he moved or spoke. "I watched you tonight. You're so like her." His voice was low, now only mildly slurred.

Another silence followed. She cleared her throat. He reached and touched her arm resting on the seat divider. She didn't move until he tightened his grasp and pulled her roughly into his arms. He hugged her hard for a long time. She was frightened. She could smell whiskey, and garlic from the meatballs. "She was a lovely, lovely woman. A lovely, lovely human being." After a sigh sounding close to a moan, he abruptly released her, lurched from the car and disappeared into the hotel lobby.

Back at home, she found her father sitting in the living room, sipping a brandy. She could see food and unwashed dishes still cluttering the dining table and kitchen counters. Half-filled glasses sat in wet rings on end tables, coffee tables, the piano, the mantel.

"Get Harry into his hotel all right?"

"He's there. I hope he's all right." She glanced again at the mess of the house. "I'm tired," she said, wondering why he hadn't done a thing. "I'll clean up in the morning."

"Shouldn't we put away the perishables?"

Mark, coming into the room, said, "I'll handle it, Amber. Go to bed. You've done enough."

As she moved toward the staircase, she lifted a copy of Harry Biggs' book. It was a thin volume called *Muted Sorrows*. Once in bed, she read the bio on the back cover, noticing that he'd graduated from Xavier, the school her mother had attended. The dedication read "To my beloved better half," which seemed to refer to a wife, though she was sure her father had described Harry as a middle-aged bachelor.

Though poetry at this point in her life tended to confound her, this book was surprisingly accessible. There were only 72 pages, and she read quickly. When she came upon a poem called "Feeding Poets," she slowed down, read and reread—then reread again. It involved a cocktail party for three poets, a reading—a party only a bit bigger than the one she'd prepared tonight. The scene through the poem was all too familiar, yet it was the closing lines that caught her full attention:

> Now the poets gather
> at her table.
> She feeds them better than
> they feed themselves.
> Amid a symphony
> of hollow words,
> her silence speaks
> the rhetoric of grace.
> She moves and serves

amid the glow of stars,
quietly giving, giving,
without return.

Amber sat rigid in her bed, turning over the enigmatic phrases, staring out at falling snow shimmering in the light of a neighbor's porch—a cold, enchanted, perplexing world.

New Year's Eve came and went. Her father hosted a modest-sized party of friends, though Mark returned to law school ahead of it.

As soon as it could be arranged, Amber packed her things and left for the university.

THE GYPSY

Ben Brown had walked the neighborhood for many years, and in spite of dizziness that wearied him, he kept on. Today, he sat on the front porch to put on his walking shoes, setting his slippers close to the door. It was spring of an election year…a boisterous blue flag up the street, opposition signs in other yards—a world divided, faltering, led by men as old and infirm as he.

He'd been born in this house eighty some years ago, gone away to college and lived away until a year into his marriage to Grace. Then his parents had moved south, and he'd bought the place and stayed on—for the rest of his life, as it was turning out. The house, precisely built by a Dutch master carpenter, had a pool in the back yard, a large garden, tall cedars for privacy. He loved this small, quiet piece of the world, even though it was fast becoming too much for him. He'd taught in a nearby high school. Their only child, a son Sam, lived across the country, as did three grandchildren whom they saw once or twice a year. His wife lamented the distance but wouldn't move to Los Angeles, wouldn't leave this peaceful haven for any reason.

The neighborhood had miles of sidewalks and a park with a wide river, bike and walking paths, and acres of green expanse. The streets were so familiar he traveled them in his sleep. He could feel (he imagined) a groove he'd worn in the aging sidewalks. It was April. Huge old trees were alive and bright with unfurling leaves, and friendly tulips nodded to him as he passed. It had rained in the night, and the grass was still wet, the air fresh and brisk. He wore baggy jeans that gradually slipped down his shrinking hips, and a green, untucked flannel shirt.

"It's only me, Norman," he said to a Golden who barked whenever he passed. He knew the dogs. They ignored him for the most part, as did the young women with strollers, talking on cell phones as they went by. He never carried a phone, never wore a headset for music, and could not understand why everyone did these days. Wasn't it neighborly to speak?

His legs on the long, slow ascent from the river began to feel crushingly tired. He slowed his pace. The dizziness intensified—some inner ear problem, he'd been told—so he reversed directions, turning downhill, crossing a busy street into the park. There was a bench nearby, and he sat down to rest.

Ben read even more than he walked. At unpredictable moments book characters wandered into his head. Today, it was Billy Pilgrim, a man with no control over where he was in time. Ben related to the problem. He considered Billy an old and sympathetic friend.

Above the bench stood a fluffy locust tree; he looked up directly into sunlight filtering through the lacy leaves, and the tree and bench began to whirl. He averted his eyes, leaned forward, and stared at the ground, trying to regain his equilibrium. Ben fixed on one yellow dandelion bloom, and the world slowly stilled. He felt sick to his stomach, but it passed in a few moments.

He closed his eyes and momentarily dozed off but was jolted by a pack of runners, high school boys training for cross country. They were following a course marked with a chalk line around the park. The boys looked familiar to him. Gathering energy from their presence, he stood and walked after them, and soon began jogging, but instead of turning toward the river as they did, he crossed the busy street into his neighborhood. He broke into a run. The houses had a young look, as did the half-grown trees. A bumper sticker on a parked car spelled out "I LIKE IKE" in red, white, and blue.

He ran for several miles before turning toward home. When he arrived his tee shirt was wet, his hair windblown and full of curls. On his front porch stood their neighbor, ringing the doorbell, obviously distressed. She lived just across the street in a tiny, two-bedroom rental house. She was dark and gypsy-like with some sort of accent. His mother thought she was Romanian. Another neighbor, the old man two doors down, had told him she was a witch. Her name was Tatiana. She was, he guessed, in her early thirties—a small, lithe, athletic creature with flashing dark eyes and long black hair.

"Is your father home?" she asked anxiously.

"My parents are in Mexico. I'm here by myself. Is something wrong?"

"I think someone has broken into my house."

"Oh, no!" he exclaimed—with genuine concern. "Should I call the police?"

"No police, please, unless necessary. I hoped your father might come in with me. Maybe you would do it instead. I'm afraid to go inside alone."

"Sure," he said, not all that convincingly. He followed her across the street and examined the side door. It was open but didn't appear damaged.

"I just came home from work. The door was like this. I have not gone in. There is not much to steal."

"Let's see." He stepped in ahead of her, went into the kitchen and looked around. She came up beside him and took his arm. "Please, let's check the rooms," she said.

A guest bedroom with a bare single mattress, her own bedroom clean but spare, a bathroom, a pantry, two closets...no one was there. "The basement," she whispered and led him down a stairway with a turn in it, lighted only by a bare bulb at the top. He filled with apprehension as they descended into the dark, damp space. She searched for a ceiling light with a pull chain, located it, and the drab room dimly appeared, and yet corners and a second room, a former coal cellar, remained dark. He cautiously looked behind the sprawling furnace, poked into the coal cellar and behind a pile of boxes, finding no one. Then a box fell, unnerving them both. She cried out, but he saw it was nothing and returned the box to the pile.

"No one here," he said with relief.

"Thank you for your bravery," she said sincerely. "I never leave that side door open. I don't know what happened, unless it was the shadows." She shut off the light and followed him up the stairs. She sat down at her kitchen table and motioned him to join her. "Would you like a glass of wine?" When he hesitated, she said, "Maybe orange juice. I see you running all the time, keeping in good shape. Wine would be breaking training."

"One glass wouldn't hurt," he said, wondering what the shadows were.

Long before infirmities, he'd hiked the park in all weather, rediscovering the quiet places he'd known as a boy, passing benches occupied by old men. He'd cross the busy street and hurry uphill toward his house. Once they'd moved in, Grace had loved the pool most of anything. She was an accomplished swimmer and often in the evenings swam naked. He joined her, of course, and the darkness and thick cedars inspired much freedom of expression.

He planted gardens, more every year; she especially loved purple dragon. They had a child, a boy, and the enchanted evenings in time came to an end. He still lived them in dreams.

On the bench, steadying himself with his hands, he thought again of Tatiana. His parents, both in the ministry, had traveled to Chiapas, visiting the denomination's missionaries. They had trusted him to stay alone—he had just turned seventeen—with his grandmother looking in on him and bringing food every other day.

The night was dark with no moon; he was reading in the den when the knock came. It was too late for someone to be stopping by. He glanced through a small window beside the door and saw the gypsy. He'd been in her house just hours before, so he opened to her.

"I'm sorry," she said. "It's late. Could you come over and be with me a little while? I'm still frightened."

"I guess I could." He set down his book, locked the door, and followed her across the street.

She ushered him in through the same side door, and they both sat at the kitchen table. The light was faint. He looked through her front window; his house was ablaze compared to hers. She stiffened as light and a shadow moved across her wall and disappeared at the corner.

"The shadows visit me. I think they are shadows of the people who lived here before me."

"The Mortons? They died in a plane crash."

"Their shadows come to me. The dead seek me out. My grand-parents were gypsies, so I know. I don't invite the shadows. I don't want them."

Again, a shadow moved across the wall and disappeared.

"I think it's just car lights passing the side of your house—shining through your tree and making shadows."

She stared at the wall and watched it happen again as a car passed. "You must think I'm very superstitious."

The shadow came again, but there was no car. He puzzled about it and felt chilled and more sympathetic. "Not at all. Something is strange. Come back to my house for a while."

"I have to get to bed. I work early tomorrow. Is there an extra bedroom?"

"Oh," he said, surprised. "You want to sleep there?"

"Just for one night if it isn't an imposition."

It wasn't. One night turned into two, then three, until close to his parents' return. She hadn't known there was a pool. They swam each night in the dark. She called him a beautiful boy and slept with him in his bed. He lost his unwanted innocence to her breathtaking passion. When he admitted she was his first, she seemed inspired, wrapping him in her arms and legs as if trying to possess him entirely. He felt something for her—an affinity of spirit, if not exactly love. Though three nights ended it, she occupied his mind…her small, lithe body, her pointed breasts, her boyish hips… for a lifetime. She'd moved away within a few weeks. The place proved difficult to rent. Tatiana, he later learned, meant fairy queen.

One particular day, he remembered, had been too warm for early June, yet he'd labored the mile to the high school where he'd taught English for many years. Students were in their final week. He didn't go inside, knowing almost no one, but strolled the grounds, skirting the baseball field, glancing at girls playing tennis nearby. He was thinking about a story called "The Swimmer," a memory prompted by satellite images shown him the day before by a man selling safety covers for pools. The area, he could see from the images, was marked by an astonishing number of back yard pools, enough to swim in for miles— perhaps even across an entire county as the story's main character had done. Ben's students hadn't connected well with the story. They were too young to understand the tragic waste of a life unwisely lived.

He'd made his share of unwise choices, but looking back with regret was something he rarely did. He'd lived his life without much glory or disaster, with his own measure of good fortune (he thought of the gypsy…then of his wife, his best friend, whom he'd met by chance in a used book shop).

His father, who'd died at ninety, had envisioned his son following him into the ministry, but the life required more than Ben could ever give. He was more solitary and selfish than his father, more misanthropic, and above all, due to broad and habitual reading, far more secular. He'd followed his own desires, and his father, that good man, hadn't stood in his way. Ben had tried to do the same with his own son, who now wrote crime shows for television. When they were together, they mostly talked about books they'd read and the grandchildren. He wished they had more in common.

How many miles had he walked in his life? He knew this neighborhood like a beloved book. Today, it was sweltering, the first part of July. He moved through the park, crossed to his street, and wearily passed the house next door to his. The family there was black, and, unlike their white neighbors, hung out on the front porch instead of the back deck. Sarah, the wife, was always friendly, always had a child on her lap.

"Hi, there, Ben," she said. "Walking again. You're the walkin' man."

She made him smile. "Hello, Sarah. Yeah, I've walked around the world once or twice, I think."

She laughed at that.

"Please use the pool today," he said. "I'll leave the gate unlocked."

"I think we might. That's kind of you, Ben."

"I hate to see it going to waste."

"How's Grace doing?" she asked

"Oh, some days are good, some not so good."

"Let me know if you need any help."

The thing about Sarah was she meant what she said. His wife had Parkinson's and struggled with basic things. Sarah made them meals— seeming to know just when they needed them. Grace had done the same for years for ailing folks at church. Women were better at compassion than men; he delivered most of her meals and in turn received the thanks she alone deserved. He had gained immensely in the eyes of others by association with his wife.

That afternoon he sat by the pool while Grace rested inside, and Sarah and her three kids splashed about. Sarah was just a touch heavy, with beautiful honey-bronze skin. Her kids were darker, like her husband. In spite of their forty years age difference, Ben was half in love with her. He sat in a patio chair, watching them, wishing she could see the former glory of his gardens, the thick, precisely trimmed cedars now grown too tall to manage, too old and thin, some of them dying. He poured lemonade for all of them. They sat listening to the heavy rhythm of drums from the park—a Native American powwow just beginning. After some cookies, Sarah made the children pick up every plastic shark, every ball and toy boat before they left. She was remarkable.

The October colors were so glorious that Grace walked with him down to the edge of the park. She held his arm tightly because her balance was worse than his. They saw the place they'd picnicked for so many years, celebrating the day they'd fallen in love. Nothing much had changed there. A small carnival and food trucks were setting up for the weekend. Closer to the river, a dozen or so open-carry enthusiasts had gathered with their guns and families to hear speeches. Events, especially carnivals, seemed to bring a darker brand of character to the park. A year ago, a man's body had been found in the river near this spot. He'd lived under a viaduct of the nearby highway.

They sat for a few minutes on a bus stop bench. They didn't cross the busy street. "When Sam was four, we played pretend baseball on that Little League field," she said.

"I remember."

"So much life has happened here."

Death, too, he thought, but didn't say it.

Her home care nurse was coming soon, so after a short, quiet space of sunlight and golden trees, he helped her to her feet, and they began the uphill journey back. She was getting weaker. It exhausted her. He got her into her leather recliner with her feet up before the militia arrived.

The nurse, a rough-edged woman named Chloe, assisted Grace while Ben read or wrote or worked outside—until dinnertime. He took over at that point. But he couldn't heft her as Chloe could. Fortunately,

Grace was calm most evenings. She sat and talked with a small girl who sat just across from her, someone Ben couldn't see. It was her sister Prue, who had died at the age of six. Grace spoke to her calmly of dolls they had shared, identifying each by name.

The cemetery was a difficult walking distance, yet he went when he had enough strength and kept the small bed of purple dragon relatively free of weeds. But it was colder now, winter in the air, light diminishing, and he couldn't find the iron fence with all the headstones gathered inside. He could hear his heart pulsing in his ears and felt unsteady. He'd forgotten whose grave he was visiting.

An ancient black woman wandered into his mind—a frail, tiny woman who walked miles through deep woods each month to get charity medicine for her small grandson who'd swallowed lye. Her name...what was it? Phoenix, yes, like the mythical bird. Phoenix Jackson. Her mind slipping away, the old woman had imagined phantoms in her path. Still, she forged ahead, staying alive for the boy because he had no one else. No one.

His mind clicked like a camera lens; he remembered now—Phoenix was a character in a story he'd taught, but she seemed as fully flesh and blood as a beloved sister.

She evaporated, and he went on. The neighborhood he walked seemed unfamiliar. He felt anxious about it. Another election was near—signs scattered about the yards. The wind was a weary sigh, a whisper of death. Snowflakes were falling lightly. The waning sun would break through and then disappear beneath the heavy clouds.

The gypsy danced into his mind, her winsome body, her dark, flashing eyes. He also saw images of swimming pools—so many to navigate but most of them mirror-like, untouched. He saw his wife naked in the pool at night, her alabaster skin glowing in moonlight— so beautiful his heart ached. Their pool was the oldest of all in the area, the first one built, if memory served. The first one. Sarah's husband had helped him close it for the season, done most of the work. Ben warmed at the thought of such good neighbors.

It began to concern him that he didn't recognize the houses around him. They seemed smaller, shabbier than those in his neighborhood. Had he taken a wrong turn? All he had to do was find the park to get his bearings. The prevailing wind was from the west. The river was west, so he walked facing the wind. His head spun. His legs began getting heavy—heavier than they'd ever felt. His right arm was numb, perhaps from the cold. There was no bench in sight, so he sat down on someone's front porch to rest, breathing rapidly, confused and agitated.

A young woman opened the door behind him and looked out. "Excuse me, sir," she said. "Are you all right?"

"Can you tell me where I live?"

"What's the name of your street?"

He hesitated, feeling panicked. "It's slipped my mind. Somewhere close, I think."

"If my husband drives you, will you recognize it?"

He thought about that. "Yes, of course. A gypsy lives just across from me. Some people say she's a witch."

Her husband came to the door and glanced down at him. "A witch?"

She nodded, and he lifted his phone. She stepped outside, sat down beside Ben, and touched his hand. He looked at her and saw it was Tatiana.

THE IMPALEMENT ARTIST

His stage name was Professor Death, and with his target girl Selena Dubois, he served as warm-up act for the Starlight Carnival Exotic Dancers—an unusual venue for a knife thrower, though the unique nature of his act drew crowds. His birth name was Elias Hawke and Selena a less than exotic Frances Muldoon. Though she was close to forty, she was still alluring (with a tongue sometimes sharp as his knives) and doubled as a teaser opener for the strip show headliners.

Carnival people called him Professor. He had a master's degree in humanities and had once taught in a college where he discovered how far he was from true erudition. Before that, he'd spent time in the Navy. In some Eastern European port, he'd happened upon an impalement artist in a street bazaar and greatly admired the skill. Whatever one did in life, one needed to strive for perfection, he believed, so at twenty-nine, he'd quit teaching and begun studying knife throwing with The Great Lorenzo, a Barnum and Bailey circus performer. After four years of unceasing practice and mindless circus work grooming show horses and mucking stalls, he surpassed the aging master and was hired, billed as Professor Death because his targets were always live human beings.

To his misfortune, by the early 1970s circuses were dying, the circus trains being decommissioned, and he was forced to find work in a traveling carnival known as Starlight Shows. It was a humbling comedown, but his art was throwing knives, and he lived to perform. The caravan of trucks and trailers set up in small towns, often county fairs, following the seasons around the country. The locations came and went in a blur.

He'd never noticed that one of their stops was Crystal River. He hadn't been back since high school, his forgettable early life brightened only by his mother who taught him to appreciate books and his older sister who sometimes read to him. He'd lost his mother in an auto accident when he was eleven, and his father, a dairy farmer who'd never had time to develop parenting skills, had expected Elias to settle in and help run the operation. It was a job his father never escaped, even for a day. When his sister suddenly married a Marine and left town, the thought of living his life for a herd of cows drove Elias into the Navy.

His father had in time sold his farm and now lived alone somewhere to the north. Elias hadn't received this information first hand. He'd heard it in pieces from his sister who was living with her husband in Germany. She had stayed in contact with the silent, unhappy old man, about whom Elias felt remorse.

*****

Selena Dubois trusted her life to the Professor on a daily basis. He was the wisest, most steady person she knew in a world of unsteady people. The majority of carnival riffraff were in awe of him: of his intensity bordering on obsession, of his quiet intelligence, of an aura of danger and mystery setting him apart. They also went to him for help in dealing with Alfredo, the hulking, hot-headed carnival boss, who often needed guidance in the practical value of forbearance.

Elias owned many books, wrote poetry for her birthday (no one ever had), and played a guitar. It didn't hurt that he was a big, broad-shouldered man with a handsome, craggy face and long dark hair tied back. Though the two of them lived in separate trailers, they had an understanding and were looked upon as a couple by Starlight people. The arrangement, she felt, did not require strict fidelity of her, though she had higher expectations of him. She had a husband named Carl somewhere, a rattlesnake of a man, whom she'd fled from years before.

They'd arrived that morning—a Sunday—in a long caravan and a cloud of diesel fumes. It had rained hard, but now the sky had cleared, the sun steaming away the puddles from the asphalt midway. Selena was there to help unload his equipment from the back of his panel van. He was exacting about it and about the condition of his knives. He allowed no one but her to handle the props, particularly the Wheel of Death, a painted circular target board six feet in diameter, attached to a heavy metal frame on which it spun. A precise speed of spin was critical. For the climax of every act, he would strap her spread-eagled to it by wrists and ankles, set her in motion, and throw his knives from fifteen feet, a full knife's rotation, farther away than other impalement artists.

"I was born here," he said off-handedly, the two of them carefully lowering the wheel to the ground. "I showed cows at this fair."

She laughed. "This jerkwater town? You're kidding me." In a loose Starlight Shows tee shirt and fraying shorts, her long red hair pulled back and greasy from the trip, she still turned heads. "Cows? Honest to God? You'll have to show me around. People here might be shocked to know what you're doing."

"I'm an artist. They can think what they want."

"Whatever, Elias. Everybody's an artist these days. If you're one, I must be, too."

Her mockery had no visible effect on him. "You should be relieved I take my work seriously."

She bent toward him and kissed his cheek. "I know, Professor. My life depends on it."

*****

Monday showmanship events had moved slowly all afternoon. They didn't interest the girl—speed events did, though they wouldn't start until the following evening. Her name was Emma Sparrow, and she was in her Horsemaster year of 4H, her final year of fair, the climax of years of effort.

Losing patience at last, she left the arena and made for the carnival midway with her friend Tess. They both dressed the part: Western hats, halter tops, denim shorts, and short Western boots. Emma was tall with a long, oval face framed by kinky auburn hair. Some boys found her attractive, but that wasn't her concern. Tess was sturdy as a stump, rough and tumble, and tended to scare boys away, which Emma depended on. Tess ran barrels like someone demon possessed. Emma knew there were better ways.

Her quarter horse Dart belonged to her grandfather, at least on paper; the bay gelding was smart and calm, not hot and hard to handle like most barrel horses—like Tess's crazy mare Streaker. Emma had patiently trained Dart for Western pleasure, English equitation, reining, and dressage. When he was able to do all she asked of him—including flying lead changes, spins, and sliding stops—they turned finally to barrel racing. Dart was fast but their fine-tuned athleticism won their races, and they both loved the hell-for-leather events. Dart was her best friend, her obsession. She'd spent more hours with him than with any human being. She found him far more attentive and dependable.

The carnival was a new one this year, the Ferris wheel a giant double, the bumper cars not so banged up—the overall feel less trashy than usual. There were features the town had never seen before, specifically a freak show and the Starlight Exotic Dancers. Tess stopped Emma in front of a narrow stage that previewed strippers at intervals through the day and evening. A billboard blared in bold letters THE SEDUCTIVE KNIVES OF PROFESSOR DEATH. A garish painting on a large section of canvas presented the target girl in two revealing wisps of silk, spread eagled on the Wheel of Death, and Professor Death, gripping in one hand three knives fanned like playing cards, in the other a black cape covering the lower half of his face.

"What a scam," Tess said with a laugh.

"A knife-thrower in a strip show? What for?"

"It's weird. Let's get something to eat and go find out."

Emma shrugged uncertainly. She'd never been to a strip show, though now she was eighteen and old enough. Tess was forever pushing her into things she wouldn't do by herself—something Emma valued in her.

At a local Methodist church food stand, they ordered cheese burgers and Cokes. They watched the narrow stage not far down the midway as three girls appeared in ruffled, revealing costumes to a recorded tenor sax playing "Night Train" and a barker in striped coat and red bowtie touting their very conspicuous selling points.

*****

The Professor, not in black cape as advertised but simple black tuxedo with scarlet cummerbund and bowtie, walked with easy elegance onto the stage and bowed deeply. A red velvet curtain opened behind him. Selena appeared in a flimsy two-piece silk outfit, a white top tied at one shoulder, a wrap-around blue and white Samoan sarong tied at mid hip. Her midriff and shoulders were bare, her lips blood red, her hair tied atop her head. She crossed and stood to the right of a rectangular board painted black. To her left stood the Wheel of Death.

"Gentlemen... and brave ladies," he began in his professorial voice, making note of a few women mixed among the men, and, to his surprise, two fairly young-looking girls holding Western hats on their laps, seated to the far right. The sixty folding chairs were filled, and an overflow of men stood at the back of the tent. "I am an impalement artist. I am known as Professor Death, not because I've killed but because death is a close companion with every knife I throw. My assistant, Selena, has a highly advanced awareness of her own mortality. She has heard the whisper of death many times. Yet she finds being the target of my knives a strangely seductive, unusually arousing experience."

Serena smiled and nodded in affirmation.

"Watch," he continued, "and see if you don't agree."

The act began in conventional ways with unconventional music— a record played at low volume of Beethoven's darkly solemn

"Moonlight Sonata." Selena stood sideways to the black board, and his first knife impaled a red rose she held by its stem between her teeth. The close proximity of the knife to her lips caused mild shock in the audience, a collective intake of breath. She turned her back to the board and balanced a red apple on top of her head. He split the apple with his next knife.

She turned sideways to the board again. He buried a knife in the top right of the board, and she leaned back, resting the back of her neck on the handle—assuming the classic profile pose. The Professor, briefly explaining his intent, backed up to fifteen feet—an unusual distance, requiring a full turn of the knife. Starting from her knees, he traced the front of her body upward: thighs, hips, bare belly, breasts, culminating at her neck. That knife struck and exclamations rose—the blade just inches from her pale, vulnerable throat. A final knife flew, turned once in the air, and struck her topknot. The thick, red mane of hair cascaded down behind her. The audience rewarded him with relieved applause.

Smiling, bowing, he glanced at the girls at the end of the front row. The stocky one was whistling shrilly through two fingers. The slim, pretty one looked shaken.

Serena removed the knives and carried them to him. Silks flowing with her, she glided like a white bird on her return, placing her back against the board.

The Professor set himself again at a fifteen-foot distance and spoke, not looking at the audience. "And now, gentlemen and ladies…" in deep, ceremonial tones, "…the seduction."

The knife seemed in slow motion as it sliced the air, turned over, and struck near her shoulder. The silken top fell away in a soft heap at her feet. Her full breasts, pale and pendulous, voluptuous in the light, were bare except for two small silver hearts strategically placed. The crowd was stunned into silence. Who had ever seen anything like this? The impalement artist was undressing her with knives. He heard the low murmurs of disbelief, the faint intakes of breath, and he smiled a knowing smile. Selena seemed dreamy, almost drugged. With eyes lifted, she raised her hands above her head, her breasts rising as well. In the soft spotlight, she looked like a Greek goddess carved in white marble.

The Professor waited for her breathing to calm. He lifted another knife, pausing a moment as if perhaps reconsidering, and then suddenly throwing. The blade struck the knot of her sarong. All eyes saw the silken garment flutter to the floor; faces were stunned, disbelieving. She now wore only a tiny triangle, a spangled, silver G string, her milky skin more naked than skin ever seemed. They knew this was something dangerous and strange, something no ordinary strip show ever dared—and even, perhaps, beyond all bounds of decency.

He went to her, took her hand, led her a dozen steps across stage, and carefully, lovingly strapped her to the Wheel of Death. It was erotic and unnerving. She was nearly naked, utterly vulnerable, in his power. He set her spinning—a slow, steady rotation that allowed all to see her clearly, feel her serene submission. No one made a sound.

He threw his knives at intervals, taking great care, unlike others of his art who threw as many knives as fast as they were able. He threw closer to the body than any of them, with fiercer concentration. He threw with both hands. His left traced the right side of her body, starting under an arm and moving down to her ankle. His right did the same with her other half.

The final portion was all with his right hand—working up the inside of both legs until only one target remained. He hesitated, inhaled deeply, and then threw. The shining knife buried just beneath the spot her legs joined, the silver spangled vertex.

Selena shut her eyes and moaned; everyone heard and felt it. Professor Death went to the wheel, stopped its spin, and undid her ankles and wrists. She collapsed into his arms. He gave her a moment to recover, and the two bowed deeply—to uncertain applause that soon became a standing ovation. He glanced at Selena and gave her the slightest nod. Word would spread. This week would go well.

When he looked to the far right, however, he saw that the act was not a complete success. Though her raucous friend stood whistling and applauding, the slim, pretty girl had left.

*****

She noticed him watching her ride, leaning on the fence of the practice arena. It made her uneasy. She saw him again that evening as Dart and she ran the down and back and pole bending events, winning both easily. They'd practiced far longer and harder than the others. Only Tess gave her competition, but Streaker had turned too late and wide on down and back and proved an undisciplined disaster at the intricate weave of pole bending.

She liked nights at fair the best, when the crowds had left for the carnival or for home, and she had the stable mostly to herself. She sat on a folding chair in front of Dart's stall, her first-place ribbons hanging just behind her. Dart was calm, occasionally snuffling and crunching hay. On her mind were not the wins, which she'd fully expected, but the tumult she felt from the night before—the knife thrower and his unnerving show stirring something in her she'd long tried to ignore.

As if on cue, a tall figure in jeans and a black tee shirt came toward her out of the dark fairgrounds. She knew who it was before she saw his rugged face. What was he doing? What did he want? She was afraid and wasn't sure why.

He stopped in front of her. "You and your horse are exceptional," he said with a friendly smile.

"Thanks."

"Did you train him yourself?"

"Of course."

"I used to help with circus horses. I've seen the dedication it takes. You two move with one mind. It's beautiful to watch."

Taken aback by his kind words, she went silent. When he began to walk away, she said, "You're the knife thrower."

He stopped and turned. "I am. And you're the girl who left before the end."

122

She felt her face flush. "I'm sorry…you were very good. I'm not sure why I did. The show was fascinating, but also kind of…well…"

"Disturbing?"

She hesitated, and then nodded.

He looked at her with sympathetic eyes. "I throw knives for the same reason you ride the way you do. I want to be the best anyone can be. Doing it to open a strip show changes things—I've never done anything like it before. The domination and submission stuff attracts strange people."

"Your target girl seemed turned on by it."

He laughed quietly. "Mostly acting."

They both fell silent. She searched for something to say. "Have you worked in this town before?"

"No, but I was born here—haven't been back in years."

She brightened. "Born here? And you actually escaped this place? Wow, that's good to know."

He folded his arms, quiet for a moment, as if measuring her words. "So, you race again tomorrow night?"

She nodded.

"I'll try to be there. My name is Elias Hawke."

She shook his outstretched hand. "Emma Sparrow."

He smiled. "Birds of a feather." He let go of her hand, turned toward the midway and walked off. She stood, a bit dazed, reaching for Dart's forehead and absently stroking it.

*****

Elias returned to a crisis. Douglas, the English dwarf who counted money and kept books for the carnival, had just lost all his wages and some of the day's take in a poker game, and his wife Artemus, the bearded lady, had bloodied his nose. She'd also made the mistake of telling Alfredo, who blew up and fired him—not at all what she intended. Alfredo was fuming to begin with—Selena had been seen going off on the arm of a customer after the show, breaking a cardinal rule. Elias managed to sort out half the problem by lending Douglas money and getting him rehired by threatening to quit, and the other half by assuring Alfredo he'd handle things with Selena. Alfredo, a creature of strong impulses, felt no disgrace in bowing to the persuasiveness of the Professor. His employees considered it shrewd business.

Elias stopped by Selena's trailer and knocked. When she didn't answer, he returned to his place, opened a beer, and began playing his guitar, an old Gibson bought from a trapeze artist in the Barnum and Bailey days. He enjoyed playing, sometimes even inventing songs and lyrics and writing them down. It was an escape from the intensity of the knives and a surreal work life. He was opening another beer when Selena knocked and came in. She looked troubled, not her usual upbeat mood after some male admirer had talked her into a drink.

"Alfredo is boiling. He saw you go off with a local. I told him I'd take care of it."

Her face reddened. "Fuck Alfredo. That fat Dago doesn't run my personal life." His presence, as always, began to calm her. She softened her tone. "Anyway, he can relax. It wasn't what he thinks— just a guy from my past."

Elias handed her a beer. "What guy?"

"A guy I knew in high school. Quite a surprise."

"You don't seem all that happy about it."

"My past wasn't all that happy." She flopped down on the small couch next to him. "Just play me something nice. I need to chill. Maybe I'll stay the night if it's okay."

"It's always okay," he said, and began playing "Blackbird." She sat back in the corner of the couch, sighed, and closed her eyes.

*****

She saw him at every one of her shows. Only her grandparents were as faithful. He'd stop afterwards at Dart's stall and talk in his engaging way. They both were readers and shared a passion for Tolkien. As a headliner, he did only three shows a day, so when he wasn't practicing, he had some time and saved it for her.

On Friday evening, they walked away from the fairgrounds. He wanted to see the town he'd been gone from for eighteen years (making him about thirty-six, she estimated, though he seemed younger). She watched him closely as he noticed landmarks gone: a saddle maker's store now a vacant lot, a bicycle shop remade into a law office. He seemed mildly dismayed at the changes. She learned he'd been in the Navy, had taught in a college, had worked in a circus, had experienced more of life than she probably ever would. She'd never met anyone so mysterious, so interested in her, so quiet and collected, so wise. She wondered about his relationship with his target girl, and fantasized about the role.

As they reached the end of the street, where a bridge crossed the river, he stopped her and looked around. The town was so familiar to her she hardly saw the grimness of this east end, the empty buildings marked with "condemned" and "no trespassing" signs.

"There was a drugstore here once," he told her, indicating the brick building with plywood-covered windows. He pointed across the bridge. "I see the dancing school is still there."

Across the river stood Sally's Ballet and Tap, a one-story cement block structure that needed paint. "My mother started ballet there," she said.

He paused and looked up at a streetlight that had just come on. "Honestly? What was her name?"

"Back then it was Maggie Brown."

He laughed and crossed his arms. "Maggie Brown was your *mother*? Good Lord. She was the Strawberry Festival Queen—back in my time."

"You actually knew her?"

"Well…I wanted to. She was the town beauty. And you're her daughter! Imagine it!"

Emma felt a moment of uncertainty. She wasn't sure how to interpret the reverence in his tone.

He went on. "I was maybe twelve when she was Strawberry Queen. She didn't know I existed." He grew quiet and seemed to be sorting through files in his mind. "There was one experience I should tell you about." He put his hands in his pockets and glanced up at a sky bright with carnival lights and then down at a boarded window. "It was right here—in the drugstore. It had a soda bar. I remember I was drinking a cherry coke and looking out the window at the river. It was fall and getting dark early. Your mother came out of the dancing school carrying a tote bag. The moon was full, and when she passed under the streetlight, she put down her tote and began to dance to some kind of music in her head. When she finally stopped, all the ice had melted in my cherry coke. It was magic. I've never forgotten it. And now this strange serendipity! I thought you were familiar, but now I know why."

Could she take him seriously? "My mother and I aren't anything alike."

"I disagree. In important ways you are—your grace at your art, your dedication to it. Your beauty."

She wanted to believe him but her voice didn't convey it. "She was much prettier than I am. She was a great dancer. But then she got married and became a missionary."

"Ah. Not what I'd imagined."

"She married a minister named John Sparrow—my father. He took her to India, and they built a school. They've lived there ever since, doing humanitarian things for poor people, but they left me at home."

She felt his eyes examining her. Her face flushed.

"You don't sound pleased about it."

"My grandparents raised me. They gave me Dart. They've been good to me."

"But you were left behind."

She shrugged. "I went to India once and hated it, hated the poverty. They sent me home to grow up on a farm and go to good schools."

"Without them."

She sighed and touched his arm. "I didn't mean to get into this. I feel like a selfish bitch just talking about it."

He smiled sympathetically, and then motioned toward the lights. "It's late. I've kept you way too long."

She nodded, but it wasn't what she wanted to hear. Together, they moved toward the fairgrounds. He slipped an arm through hers, and she trembled, beset by unsettling thoughts, not wanting to leave him. She pressed his arm tightly to her side. She couldn't begin to read his mind. Could he read hers?

Though she'd known him less than a week, she could imagine him undressing her with his knives. She could imagine him strapping her to the Wheel of Death. She could imagine trusting him with her life.

*****

On Sunday Starlight Carnival was moving on to some town in northern Ohio. He despised Saturday nights and refused to work the show. Alfredo called it Red Hot Ramble. Depending on the town and the local police, the show was double admission and no holds barred. The strippers hated what they had to do but loved the money. Many had been groped, violated with fingers, tongues, and teeth, even bloodied with fingernails. A few had landed in jail for lewd and lascivious behavior. To his bewilderment, Selena always worked the Ramble.

That morning, Emma Sparrow had been awarded the high point trophy for speed. That afternoon, she'd ridden a choreographed Horsemaster demonstration to music—a ballet of horsemanship that made him emotional to watch. In the middle of the piece, she had removed Dart's bridle and bit, and worked him only with her legs— spins in both directions, flying lead changes, sliding stops, long, elegant patterns. He'd never seen the like of it; it was a level of skill that few ever reached. In her he'd found a kindred spirit as artist. But he was drawn as well to her youth, her beauty, to the purity of her goals. She was too young for him, he knew, and he took care not to overstep. Some things were wiser left in dreams.

That evening, as the Red Hot Ramble got underway, he spent his time helping move Dart from the stables back to the farm. Her grandfather was there to assist. Oliver Brown was a thin, spry man in his seventies who remembered the Hawke dairy farm and Elias's father. Her grandfather didn't presume to take charge of Dart. That was Emma's territory. The big animal stepped lightly into the trailer at her bidding. She owned an old Ford pickup into which Elias and Oliver loaded tack, hay bales, ribbons, trophies, riding costumes. She wore jeans, a tee shirt, and tall muck boots for a final cleaning of the stall. Elias rode with her to the farm, the horse trailer clattering behind. Oliver drove his own truck.

The farm was modest: a barn and small stable, aging white clapboard house with a large front porch and red roof. Oliver, now in semi-retirement, leased his fields to neighbors.

Dart ran happily into the pasture to see his partner horse; he nuzzled her and began telling her (Emma explained) the whole story of fair. Elias was charmed. They unloaded the truck, and he sat for a few minutes and had tea in their cluttered farm kitchen. The green smell of the place was the scent of his childhood. Emma's grandmother was a large woman, pleasant enough, but she seemed rightfully wary of him. They'd heard he was a knife thrower working for the carnival and agreed it was an unusual occupation. He made no attempt to explain his life choices.

Emma soon after unhitched the horse trailer, changed from muck boots into sneakers, and drove him back to the fairgrounds. As she pulled up beside his travel trailer, he said, "If you'd like to come in, you can see how I live. It's very Spartan."

"I like things simple," she said.

She followed him in and sat down on his couch. He wondered if it was wise having her here. She saw his guitar and asked if he played. He nodded. His small kitchen had nothing on the countertops. Everything was tied down or put away, ready for travel.

"You told me you have books," she said.

He motioned her toward his small bedroom, filled wall to wall with a double bed. He pulled out one large, built-in drawer from beneath the bed, then another. The drawers were filled with books, spines upward.

"I have a cabin in Wisconsin. Most of my books are there."

"Does someone live here with you?"

"Why would you ask?"

"I was wondering about your target girl."

"Selena? She's a friend. She has her own place."

"I thought she might be more than that. Your act is very intimate."

He closed the book drawers and returned to the couch. "Yes, it is. We've been partners for about a year. She's had to learn to trust me."

"I can see that." She sat down beside him. "I'd like you to throw knives at me."

Her request didn't shock him. "I've been asked before. The answer is no. It's not something I do for fun."

"I wouldn't be doing it for fun."

He looked hard at her. She was serious. "There's no time, Emma. We leave in the morning."

"Elias..." It was one of the few times she'd called him by name. "What is going on? Why are you so interested in me?"

He looked down at his folded hands. "I admire your artistry."

"That's all?"

He hesitated. "No, it's not all, but you're half my age, Emma."

"It doesn't matter to me."

"It matters to me. And you know I live the life of a nomad. I'm migratory, a hummingbird."

"I don't care."

He laughed and touched her hand. "I have nothing to offer you. We need to say goodbye. Maybe we'll meet again next summer."

"My 4H days are over. I won't be here."

He shrugged. "A star-crossed romance, then."

"We haven't had a romance!" She got to her feet and began to pace in front of him. "I wish you weren't such a gentleman. You've barely touched me! Don't you know how much I care about you? I'm not a child, Elias!"

Her honest, impassioned words moved him. Though he required a few moments to absorb them, he finally said in a low voice, "I know you're not a child, Emma," and rose to his feet. "I consider you more than my equal. I apologize. I've been afraid of spoiling everything."

"You won't spoil anything." She stepped toward him.

Knowing better, knowing enough to stop, he nonetheless reached out and brushed her cheek with his fingertips, touched her tangled hair, and, with a heavy sigh, pulled her into his arms. Her inexperience was touchingly obvious, but she followed his lead, doing what he did, moaning softly at times, tears filling her eyes.

The distant, tinny blare of the Red Hot Ramble serenaded them from across the midway.

*****

It was near midnight, Selena had survived the show, and wrapped in a red satin robe was making her way to her trailer. The herd of human swine was gone and good riddance. It was late, but a light was on in Elias's trailer. A pickup truck she didn't recognize was parked nearby. She knocked, but he didn't answer, and though she felt jittery, in need of his presence, she turned toward her own trailer, passing by Alfredo whose face glowed with venal delight.

"Raunchiest Ramble ever," he said to her. "Biggest take of the year. And nobody arrested!" He laughed and continued toward his long trailer where he'd no doubt be celebrating with someone— thankfully, not her.

She'd left a light on, yet her trailer was dark. She didn't scare easily, but she didn't like coming home to darkness. Ghosts of the past visited her in such moments. Tonight, though, she was worn to the bone and needed sleep. She put her key in the lock, but the door swung open by itself. She dimly saw a large hand floating in the air in front of her. It struck her in the face like a hammer. A bomb exploded inside her head, a low voice rasped like a bad phone connection, and then black silence.

*****

Elias sat hours at her bedside. Selena was conscious but hadn't spoken in three days. Emma had been the one to discover her as she left his trailer after midnight. Her truck lights had revealed a body in a puddle of blood just outside her open door, her face beaten beyond recognition. Elias had heard Selena's knock earlier but hadn't answered. He felt guilty, remorseful. Emma seemed in shock.

He refused to leave with Starlight Shows, was staying on until Selena recovered enough to travel. Alfredo grudgingly agreed yet turned nasty when he began weighing the consequences of being without his most lucrative act. Multiple times he reminded Elias of their binding contract.

Emma talked her uneasy grandparents into allowing Elias to move their two trailers to the farm, close to the barn and electrical hookups.

Some days she went with him to the hospital. He found her a comfort and a concern. Selena's nose and one cheekbone were fractured and eyes blackened, swollen shut. Much of her face was wrapped now, less horrific than at first. The attack had been vicious. It would take time and surgery to restore her face, he was told. The police had no real leads and were waiting to hear her story. Elias had some thoughts but didn't voice them.

He took time to unload his target boards from the panel van and set them up in the barn. The light wasn't all that good, but the floor was concrete, a solid base.

He practiced throwing his knives during her work hours. They had not resumed their lovemaking. Emma's mood was somber. His world had touched hers in a dark and ugly way, and he felt responsible. Still, she wanted his company and seemed to value this unexpected time they'd been given.

*****

Emma taught at a local boarding stable four hours a day—mostly adolescent girls who adored horses but not the hard work needed to ride well. Their attitudes frustrated her. She half-heartedly thought about college. Her 4H life with Dart was over. She still worked with him early every morning, often before Elias was awake. It was habit: figure eight patterns endlessly repeated. They seemed to embody her life, her future.

On Sunday morning, with her grandparents away at church, she went looking and found him practicing in the barn.

She watched for a few minutes, admiring his skill. "I want to be your target," she told him.

He stopped throwing and turned to her. "I've already said no."

"Is Selena's costume in her trailer?"

"If you're thinking of wearing it, forget it. The costume is a trick. She'd have to demonstrate. I hit close to the knot and she touches a button. Presto, her clothes are on the floor."

"Honestly? How disappointing."

"Well, everything else is legitimate. You can't go slicing up costumes on a daily basis."

His knives were spread out like cards on a small table. She picked one up. "I want to feel what it's like to be your target girl."

He took the knife away and laid it back in place. "Selena will be back working soon enough. I don't need another target girl."

"Please, just once—on the Wheel of Death."

"No."

"I'm not afraid. I trust you. I just want to feel what Selena feels."

"Selena's done it so many times she doesn't feel anything."

132

"I don't believe you. You practically make her your slave."

He snorted. "She's an actress."

"Put me on it, please."

*****

He moved toward the wheel, brusquely motioning for her to follow. "Take off the shirt and jeans. I might put holes in them."

Without hesitation, she stripped to her underwear, and he strapped her wrists and ankles to the wheel. The sight of her young body was dizzying.

He felt her watching everything he did—with great interest. "This is very sexy," she said.

"Yes." He leaned in and lightly kissed her. "But that might change."

"I can't imagine it."

He kissed her again, set the wheel slowly spinning, and moved to his knives. At this moment, above all, he needed absolute focus. Her body was a target, nothing more. There was too much at stake. He threw four knives quickly, very close to her torso. He moved to her legs, traveling up and down the outside, close to the skin. He aimed at last at the inside of her calves, threw once, threw again, and she cried out, "Stop this thing! Stop it!"

He smiled faintly, went to her and brought the wheel to a halt. Her face was drained of color, her eyes distressed. He knew the symptoms well. He released her wrists and ankles, saw the line of blood pooling on the inside of her calf.

She collapsed, and he helped her to a bench. The wound, he knew, was superficial. He wiped away the blood and bandaged it. She breathed heavily, miserably.

"You cut me."

"I told you this was dangerous."

"I trusted you! I hate that damned wheel!" She rose, rushed into an empty livestock stall, and vomited.

*****

A telegram for Elias arrived at the farm two weeks after Selena's assault. He read it but not aloud. He said to her simply, "I can't wait for Selena. Things are coming apart. They need me back." The hospital, he'd already told her, was releasing Selena sometime the following week.

The next morning, she rode Dart early. On her return to the stable, she found a note tacked to the gatepost of Dart's stall. She read it, not believing he'd leave without seeing her. It said, simply, "Emma. You are wonderful. Thank your grandparents for their gracious hospitality. Selena will be taking her trailer as soon as she's out of the hospital. I won't ever forget you. Your devoted admirer, Elias."

She was still in a moody daze three days later when she picked up Selena from the hospital and drove her to the farm. Selena chattered on as if she hadn't spoken for months.

"They're in Goshen, Indiana, some big county fair," she said. "Elias says he's getting me a feathered Mardi Gras mask for the act till my face looks halfway decent, if it ever does."

Emma glanced at her, nodding. Selena's face was a yellowish purple, swollen and hard to look at. "He's a good man. Way better than that two-bit carnival deserves. He cares about us—freaks and all—looks after us…stands up to that bastard of a boss."

"I know he's a good man."

Selena looked over at her and then went silent for several minutes. "Ever think of being a target girl?" she asked at last.

Emma laughed sharply. "I went on the Wheel of Death a few days ago. I got sick as a dog."

Selena grinned. "I puked for a week trying to ride that damn thing. Finally started taking Dramamine."

"Did he ever cut you?"

Selena frowned and shook her head. "Elias? He never misses."

"Well, he cut me."

"He never misses, honey. If he cut you, he must've meant to."

This jarred her. "Why would he?"

"How the hell should I know?" She went silent a moment, thinking. "Why were you on the wheel? Something happen between you two I don't know about?"

Emma hesitated. "I guess so."

Selena looked doubtful. "Hmm. You're way too young for him."

"Probably."

"Listen, before this shit happened to me, I'd have torn your eyes out. But…now I guess it doesn't matter."

"Why say that? He's waiting for you."

"Do me a big favor, honey. Get a message to him. Just tell him I have to go away. I need a place to disappear. I have some ideas about where, but I'm not telling a soul.   Mention the name Carl, and he'll understand."

"Carl?"

"Yeah—someone you never want to meet."

Selena thanked Emma's grandparents and was gone with truck and trailer within half an hour. Later, as her grandfather sat with her at the kitchen table waiting for dinner, he said, "Elias seemed like a decent man, but what a strange life. I don't understand it. He could have had a big dairy farm."

Emma fidgeted with her napkin. "Farming wasn't his passion. But he's done so many interesting things, Gramp. Now he wants to be the world's best knife thrower." She felt odd saying it. He nodded and smiled; she was sure he could see right through her.

Her grandmother reached in front of her with a bowl of mashed potatoes. "The world's best knife thrower…God knows what for," she said. "Honestly, those carnival people are a peculiar lot. It's not a life I'd want. Mean and rootless. Living in trailers. No kind of life at all."

*****

She spent a long, restless night, full of dreams of being lost in a strange city. She rose at daybreak to ride her horse. There was a cool breeze, trees twisting and clouds rolling into one another. She had in mind a long trail ride around the farm. She needed time to think about

135

all that churned inside her—about his leaving without seeing her, about the cut on her leg (already healed). What had actually happened between them? Scattered and perplexing memories tumbled in her head. She thought of her mother, the beauty queen, leaving her life and following a man to India.

She pushed Dart to an easy canter, ran a hand along his powerful neck, feeling delight in the smooth, muscular surface. At the same time, she felt her nerves tightening like the strings of a guitar. She remembered the feel of the knife-thrower's face and neck, and the caress of his hands. Gentle, knowing hands. Hands she'd felt she could trust with her life.

They entered a large, fallow clover field they'd ridden many times. She touched Dart with her heels, and he accelerated. Above, she saw a hawk circling, diving suddenly from the sky and disappearing in the trees. The sun burst above the horizon, a blinding dazzle before her. They ran straight into it.

She gave Dart his head, and instantly they were at full gallop. They both craved the insane pace. They soared. For a moment, she imagined them frozen in stride, the world rushing by them at warp speed. The illusion dissolved in the pounding of hooves as a new vision materialized. They were now accelerating like a jetliner lifting into the sky from a static and startled earth.

Both were on fire. They ran as they never had before. The faster they went, the more she sensed them closing in on something. She thought she saw glimpses of it out beyond this field and farm, beyond the horizon. It was a place of changing, blinding colors, a place of uncertainty and dreams.

She remembered the slums of Delhi and the calm of her mother in their midst—a life grim and impoverished and the beauty queen embracing it.

How odd that Professor Death should be a source of life for her. She felt amazed at such paradoxes.

At a distance, above the pounding of hooves, she heard a voice shouting her name. She came to suddenly, reined in Dart until they'd slowed to a walk. They'd nearly reached the end of the long field, and she hadn't been aware of it. She turned in the saddle and saw her grandfather, full of anxious concern, waving to her from the high seat of his tractor. "Groundhog holes in that field!" he shouted. "It's dangerous!"

"We're fine!" she shouted back.

He was a cautious man, and he looked relieved.

Silhouetted in morning light, she felt breathless, full of wild, unreasoning hope.

*****

June, 1974. London Daily Mail.

REBIRTH IN SOUTH ENGLAND.

A newly organized Austen Brothers Circus opened this week in Brighton. Their headliners are the Flying Alessandro Family, renowned aerial acrobats, and a breathtaking knife-throwing couple known as Hawke and Sparrow, (the target girl of this sexy duo is a skilled equestrian performer).

The Brighton stay of two weeks will be followed by another at Southampton. Bravo to this bold venture! E.R.

INERTIA

It is already past noon, and Max lies in his bed like a bag of sand. He feels drugged, sluggish, too heavy to sit up and swing his feet to the floor. The room is hot, his tee shirt damp at the neck, his hair oily and matted. His scalp itches, his four-day beard feels like a rash. He hasn't showered for days and lacks the energy to do it now. He recalls his father coming in early that morning, jarring him awake, and serving an ultimatum: "Get off your ass and get a job, goddammit, or get out. I'm fed up."

His father slams the door and leaves to install a water heater or snake a hairball from a drain. He is pushing Max to apprentice with him in the plumbing trade, but Max has no interest. He has no interest in much of anything. He sometimes thinks a girlfriend would help his state of mind, but that would require effort and money. He can't even afford a cell phone, which isolates him from almost everything and everyone. His parents recently cancelled their landline, probably to send him a message. His mother used to put beer in the refrigerator for him but doesn't any more. He borrows her computer sometimes to look for jobs, but those he's qualified for are menial and depressing. If he goes anywhere, he has to walk or endure the hassle of begging for his mother's car. He feels his life narrowing but doesn't know what to do about it. He's worried that his father's ultimatum isn't a bluff.

Max's nights and days have assumed a pattern. He stares at mindless television shows for half the night, trying to put himself to sleep. He groggily awakens at first light, still in the chair with the screen glowing. He shuts it off and drags himself upstairs to bed and sleeps until midday or later, thrashing about in dark, chaotic dreams.

He isn't taking care of himself, wears sweat pants and tee shirts instead of real clothes. He forgets to brush his teeth. In the afternoons he reads a little, mostly *Good Housekeeping* magazines and *National Geographics*, whatever is lying around, but more often he walks the neighborhood. They've lived here his entire twenty-one years, so he knows a little about the neighbors on their block. He has delivered their papers and mowed their lawns. These days he tries to avoid them because they usually ask what he's doing, and he has no honest answer. Many of them are older now; some of the houses have sold to young couples with children. His neighborhood friends are in college. Things around him are changing, but Max is not.

His mother is worried and tries hard to understand his problems, frightened that they have another child with mental health issues. She works mornings as an elementary school aide. She's usually home by the time he gets up, and she often makes him bacon and eggs. She seems to enjoy having someone to talk to, have coffee with, but she clearly wants him to get on with his life. The inertia has gone on for what—has it been three years? He's lost track of time.

During the meal, she tells him, "I've heard that Mrs. Roloff isn't doing very well. She's looking for someone to help her with the house—you know, putting up storm windows and things like that."

Max knows Mrs. Roloff. He has mowed her lawn several times. She's a former high school English teacher who reluctantly retired in her seventies—his sophomore year. When he showed up in her English class for the first time as a freshman, she mentioned what a wonderful student his sister Anna had been, not intending, he guessed, to demoralize him. Max worked hard back then, had a reputation for diligence, but Anna, four years older and the school's shining star, was beyond his reach. Still, he tried. He admired her intelligence and willpower, loved her gentle spirit, and felt deserted when she went away to Princeton on a scholarship—the first in their family to attend college.

Mrs. Roloff proved a fussy and demanding teacher, though to her credit she was passionate about literature. She occasionally praised his papers. He managed a B in spite of struggling mightily with *Hamlet* and *Return of the Native*. Max tried his best, taking AP classes, playing soccer, editing the school paper—until the start of his senior year when, learning of the near-suicide of his sister in her campus apartment, he suffered some sort of massive short circuit. He managed to graduate, primarily due to sympathetic teachers. He abandoned all college plans.

Fragile and on indefinite leave from graduate school, Anna stays for now with their grandmother in New Brunswick. The family drives there two or three times a year. She is still Anna but quieter, less sure of herself.

He cannot imagine working for Mrs. Roloff. Yet his father's threat weighs heavy on him, so he says, "Maybe I'll go talk to her some time."

"She needs somebody right away."

He feels a rush of anger. "Yeah, mom, okay. I'll do it later today."

"You should clean up first."

"I'm going to. Jeez…"

"I don't mean to be critical, but you don't smell very nice."

"God, mom, I get the point." He's embarrassed.

In the bathroom mirror he sees the reflection of a young man who could pass for a street person. The image unnerves him. He takes a half hour in the shower. He shaves and is surprised when he feels better. Maybe he'll do it again tomorrow.

At nearly five, just before his father gets home from work, he finally walks to Mrs. Roloff's house at the end of the next block. Every step is a struggle. It's a corner house with a large yard. He tries to avoid her lawn jobs because she's critical of the work he does. He wonders why one aging woman lives alone in an old Victorian house needing so much maintenance. She should be in some kind of retirement home letting other people take care of things for her. Her late husband was a college professor. She must have plenty of money.

He climbs the wood steps to a broad front porch full of weather-faded wicker furniture. A planter of spent petunias sits at the top of the steps. White paint is peeling on the doorframes. A cat has scratched deep grooves in the lower half of the door. There's work enough for five people just on the outside of the place. He feels exhausted thinking about it.

He rings the bell, rings it a second time, and finally knocks. He waits, and at last the door swings open. Mrs. Roloff stands there unsteadily with a cane. Her wispy white hair is pulled back primly in a bun. Her purple dress is crisp and neat, as if she's about to teach a class.

"Hi, Mrs. Roloff," he says.

"Oh, it's you, Max. Is something the matter?"

"My mother told me there was some work you needed help with."

She hesitates, taking a deep breath. "Oh…well, that's true. Please come in."

When he returns home, his father is in his recliner, his shoes off, reading a newspaper with a beer beside him.

Max passes by him, mentioning off-handedly, "Well, Mrs. Roloff hired me."

His father looks up from his paper with a smug smile. "Good thing," he says. "Not exactly what I'd call a job. But it'll do for now." His eyes return to his paper.

Max doesn't mention the conditions attached to his employment. The finicky old woman has made clear she has never been entirely happy with his lawn work, but she'll give him the rest of the week to prove himself. Otherwise, she'll have to look elsewhere. She wants him there at nine the next morning, and she'll have a job list for him.

He somehow shows up at her house on time, groggy and un-focused after four hours of sleep. Her commanding tone grinds him.

Though it is only early October and still in the seventies, she wants the porch furniture carried to the basement. She points the way to the basement but won't go with him. A fat orange cat stands next to her, watching him warily. She tells him she doesn't navigate stairs easily, so he'll need to find space by himself. Weary before he starts, he hauls the cushions down, and then the fraying wicker chairs. The dank basement is large, full of heaped boxes, tools, remnants of wood, junk galore, and shelves of canning jars containing inky stewed tomatoes, yellowing pickles, moldy sliced beets. A dehumidifier stands silent in a corner. Everything is damp and musty. He plugs the machine in, and, to his surprise, it kicks on. It's a small victory. In the dim light of one overhead bulb, he finds an empty back room and decides the furniture will go there.

An hour later, when the last chair is cleaned and stored, he looks into the adjoining room, finds to his surprise an elaborate model train layout covered with a thick layer of dust and cobwebs. He turns on an overhead light. The trains still sit on tracks laid on a large plywood table—027 gauge Lionels and very old. He goes to a stool in front of the transformer and switch controls, sits down in fascination, lifts a black switch engine, and blows dust from it. The wheels are rusted. He wonders if any of it works. His gloom lifts a bit. The set must have belonged to her husband who died when Max was young.

At noon, he emerges from the garage where he's found and sorted her storm windows, and she surprises him with lunch—an egg salad sandwich and a dill pickle. He's planned on lunch at home. She sits down with him and pours tea. Unused to heavy work, he is already feeling pain, especially in his back.

"This afternoon I want you to split firewood—there's an axe in the garage. When you're done, I have some things inside that need attention."

He chews his too-sweet egg salad and swallows. He takes a sip of her bitter black tea. "How long will you need me today?" She is paying him twelve dollars an hour, and he figures he's already earned what he needs.

"Until five, of course. Since there's so much to do, I want you to work full time for a while. Is that a problem?"

He hesitates just long enough to make her face tighten. "No. I was only wondering. I try to plan out my days."

In a flat voice she says, "Have you something more important to do?"

"No, I was only wondering." He glances at her, knowing he's made his first misstep.

That night at ten, after drinking (with permission) several of his father's beers, he falls into bed with every muscle screaming and blisters on both hands. His parents seem cautiously pleased with him, but this sudden move from the security of his cocoon fills him with anxiety. In spite of it, he's asleep in seconds.

Late for work the next two days, but only by fifteen or twenty minutes, he is relieved Mrs. Roloff says nothing. Her job list keeps expanding. She orders him about with her firm, chilly voice, and he cringes at the sound of it. He washes storm windows in the back yard; she makes him do half of them over again, complaining of streaks. Cursing her silently, muttering "Fussy old bitch" once she's out of earshot, he takes down screens on the ground floor and matches storms to the frames. A heavy wooden ladder gets him to the upper windows. He labors up and down until his arches throb from the rungs.

What seems weeks later, Saturday arrives, yet she still needs him a half-day to clean up her gardens. Weekend work should pay time and a half, but she never mentions it. At noon, as he's washing up at an outside spigot, she approaches him slowly, tottering across the grass with her cane, and hands him a check.

"Thank you, Max, for your work. This is pay for 35 hours."

The check is made out for $420. It's more money than he's had in a long time. "Thanks, Mrs. Roloff. See you Monday."

"Actually, I won't be needing you, Max."

He's stunned. "You mean on Monday?"

"No, I mean for good."

He wipes his wet hands on his jeans. "Uhh, I guess I don't understand."

She holds herself in a stiff, dignified way. "I think you do. This week was a trial. In five days you were twice late, and you obviously don't like the work. I want someone who sees this as a way of getting ahead. I have memories of you trying your best in school, Max, but that desire seems to be gone. I'm sorry."

He nods, not looking her in the eye, not knowing how to answer. "Sorry, too," he mumbles at last and turns towards home, humiliated. He has no idea how he'll tell his parents that he's failed in less than a week.

That night, too restless and disturbed to sleep, Max reverts to his habit of letting late night television anesthetize him. He wakens at ten Sunday morning still in the lounge chair. His parents have turned off the television and gone to church, a place he hasn't been since high school.

His father's attitude toward him has lightened through the week. His mother seems proud of him, though when he doesn't get up for work the next morning, they'll know the truth. For a moment Mrs. Roloff seems the source of all his problems. Hating her, he hauls himself from the chair and pours a cup of coffee, takes too large a swallow and burns his mouth. He spits it into the cup and cries "Shit!"

Fighting tears of frustration, he sits down at the kitchen table and stares out the window at a squirrel stuffing himself at the bird feeder. Finches wait nervously for a chance at the seeds. He wants to chase off the squirrel but can't muster the energy.

He is distracted by an idea taking shape in his head. Could he possibly go back to the old witch and beg for his job? It's desperate, but he can't think of alternatives. He has no desire to face her, let alone work for her, but the thought of being tossed out of the house alarms him.

He showers, shaves, puts on decent clothes—is out the door before his parents appear. He'll find a way to coax her into taking him back. If he needs to, he'll play on her sympathies—maybe mention Anna's struggles and even his own. He'll promise to change.

At her front door, he stares apprehensively at her doorbell, takes a heavy breath, and pushes it. He knows she is slow, so he waits and rings again. He knocks. Could she be at church? He glances at her garage and spots her Buick through a window. He knocks again. As he's about to turn and leave, he hears a faint cry that sounds like a cat. Leaning close to the door, he realizes the voice is human.

"Help me," the voice says weakly. "Help me…"

He's cornered by the cry. He wants to escape but can't. His heart racing madly, he tries the door. It's locked.

"Mrs. Roloff!" he shouts. "It's Max! I can't get in!"

"The porch light…a key," she cries out.

He reaches up, feels around the recessed top of the light and touches the key. His hand trembles as he turns the lock and enters the house. He glances anxiously around, moves toward the kitchen, and finds her lying on the hardwood floor near a grandfather clock. He rushes over and kneels beside her.

"Mrs. Roloff, are you all right?"

She touches his arm and sighs heavily. "Oh, Max… Thank heavens. I've been lying here for hours."

"What's wrong?"

"The cat got tangled in my feet. I believe I've broken a wrist. My hip is giving me pain, but I don't think it's broken. I can't seem to get up."

"I'll call an ambulance."

"Don't, please. We can do this by ourselves. My car keys are in my purse. Take them and back my car out of the garage—and get as close to the side door as possible. I want you to help me into the car and then drive me to the hospital. I'll pay you for your time, of course."

Max shakes his head, insists he won't accept pay. He takes hold of her good left arm and raises her to a sitting position. She cries out once but grits her teeth, obviously determined to make no fuss. He pulls over a sturdy oak dining chair, lifts her from behind and gets her seated in it. They both breathe heavily.

"My hip is okay," she says in a shaky whisper.

"I'll get the car."

He sits for five hours in the emergency waiting room while doctors work on Mrs. Roloff. He calls his parents from a nursing station to let them know where he is. His mother is full of questions to which he has no answers. There are no magazines to pass the time. He buys cheese crackers from a machine. An overhead television set plays a soundless football game. In a box of children's toys, he finds a book called *Where the Wild Things Are*. He sits in a chair facing away from the game and opens the book. The main character, a wild, misbehaving boy named Max, amuses him. He reads the story over and over, studying the illustrations. The simple child's book is actually about complicated things, like facing fears and mastering self. The tale is dark but ends in light—he loves it. He loves that the boy's name is Max.

When Mrs. Roloff finally appears in a wheelchair with a cast on her right forearm, she is surprised to see him.

"Good heavens," she says. "I didn't mean for you to wait."

"Nice to have some reading time."

On the drive home, she quietly explains that she has a distal radius wrist fracture. Her hip is badly bruised but intact. "Oh, why is it my right wrist?" Her voice is discouraged, emotional—a tone not typical of her. "I'm writing something, and now I'm not sure how I'll manage. I hate these limitations. Old age is a curse."

Max is not sure what to say yet attempts to be upbeat and interested. "You're writing something?"

She hesitates as if uncertain of saying more. "Oh, just a personal memoir, a family history. I'm not sure why I'm doing it. I only have a daughter, and I doubt that she'll be interested. I just want to tell the story while I'm still able."

As he turns the Buick into her driveway, she asks, "Max, why did you come to my house today?"

He stops the car close to the side door, stares at the steering wheel and waits for his anxiety to ratchet down. "I've had some problems, Mrs. Roloff, and I really need the job. I'd like another chance. Things will be different, I guarantee."

She sits a moment, considering. "I suppose that after what you've done, I can hardly refuse."

Max exhales heavily. "You won't regret it."

She reaches for the door handle with her left hand. Her voice grows commanding again. "We'll see. Now go round the car and help me into the house."

In the next two weeks, while the weather holds, he scrapes and paints the worst parts of the outside, especially door and window frames. It's messy and tedious work, but he's on time or close to it every day. Maybe it's his imagination, but the neighbors he passes on the street seem friendlier.

Mrs. Roloff is still in a lot of pain—shuffles around the house with her cane, trying to get work done with one hand, but her frustrations often bring her to tears. She still dresses smartly and somehow does her hair every day. He respects that. Each morning, she spends time at a small desk in her sewing room, struggling to type her personal memoirs on her computer using one hand. He'd like to offer help but doesn't know what he'd do. She has said nothing about being dissatisfied with his work.

Because food preparation is difficult for her, he begins making lunch for both of them. Some days he puts a frozen dinner into the oven and serves her before he leaves. She says little about this kindness but doesn't discourage it. He senses what she's feeling: the loss of independence, the forced inertia of old age. He admires the way she battles against it. He knows about inertia, and knows how little battling he's done.

She tells him her wrist is very sore and isn't healing as it should. Max drives her to the doctor, where her fears are confirmed. She is silent on the way home. As he parks near the back door, she touches his arm.

"Max, I have an idea. It may not be to your liking, but since my wrist will be an issue longer than expected, I'm afraid I'll need more help. My bedroom and bath are on the first floor, as you know. There are two bedrooms, a library, and a bath upstairs. I'd like you to consider moving in with me while I'm recovering. You'll have your choice of upstairs bedrooms. Room and board will be free, of course, and I'll pay you a salary rather than an hourly wage. I don't feel very secure by myself right now. Understand, I don't need a nurse. I'm able to handle my personal matters, so that's not an issue. You'd be free to come and go. You'd function as my handyman, cook, driver, and watchdog until I'm well again. What are your thoughts?"

Though her request seems out of the question, requiring more than he can possibly give, he asks for a day to think it over and talk to his parents. She agrees, adding, "I need you, Max. I wouldn't ask otherwise."

That evening, his parents listen as he explains Mrs. Roloff's request, and his mother startles him by voicing strong doubts about a young man caring for an old woman. Her skepticism disturbs him.

"She needs me," he says with a firmness that takes them aback. "I'll just be caring for the house, not her—doing all the stuff she can't do right now. I can handle it."

Surprised at this resolve (he surprises himself), his mother backs down without a word.

"Do it, then," his father says.

In a meek voice, his mother asks, "Will you come home and see me once in a while?"

Max laughs. "Mom, I'll only be two blocks away."

His father, far more jovial than usual, opens beers, and raises a toast to new ventures. Max, imagining life apart from his parents, feels a chill of apprehension.

The deal is settled. Mrs. Roloff seems deeply relieved. He chooses the bedroom overlooking the back gardens. The wallpaper in the room is busy with huge pink roses and tangled greenery. There's a girlish feel to the plush double bed with canopy and lacy skirt, but the arrangement is temporary, so it won't matter. The contents of his suitcase fill one drawer of the large tiger maple dresser. He opens blinds to let in some light, knowing it will take time to get used to sleeping alone in this cavernous place. A front-facing corner room turns out to be the library with walls of books and a large desk. Mrs. Roloff tells him he's welcome to read any book he wishes.

Downstairs there is one small television set rarely on. Evenings, she eats dinner on a TV tray, watching news and an occasional PBS special. Otherwise, she reads, the orange cat curled at her feet. At first, the quiet drives him to distraction. He misses the mindless comfort of his shows. He searches through her books, hoping for one that might interest him. He tries a few but can't get going with them. He asks her about the train set in the basement.

She instantly brightens. "Oh, if only you could get those trains going! They were my husband's passion. Now they're just gathering dust."

"Well, sure...I can try."

So Max's days go on, occupied with mundane, everyday work—shopping for groceries, changing cat litter, raking leaves, cleaning rain gutters—yet he likes getting up in the morning with an agenda. His evenings fill him with mild excitement. He sands and cleans and oils tracks and wheels. He suspects the transformer is dead, but he takes it apart, finds rust, leaking bushings, wire damage from overheating. He cleans and repairs it carefully. After two weeks, a passenger engine buzzes, lights up, and moves haltingly around the tracks.   Jubilant, almost giddy, he punches the air with a fist, wondering if he's inherited a touch of his father's mechanical know-how. He hasn't seen his parents since he began work on the trains.

"You're really quite handy," Mrs. Roloff says, learning of his success. They've taken to sitting at the dining table and having one drink, talking over the day. She has a small sherry; Max has a beer.

"What a surprise, huh?"

"Not really." She pauses, sips her sherry. "Are you handy at typing?"

Puzzled at the question, he shrugs and then nods.

The next morning, he follows her into her sewing room where she explains she'll dictate as he types her memoirs into the computer. For whatever reason she's chosen to trust him.

At first, he can't keep up and tells her she's made a bad choice. But she patiently slows her pace, and within a few days, they find a rhythm. The genealogy pages are dull and require concentration: great grandparents and grandparents in Germany with large farm families. She has to spell out family names for him. Her parents, however, are very different, choosing to immigrate to America as newlyweds shortly after Hitler comes to power.

When she starts telling stories of her childhood, he is spellbound. Born in Pennsylvania before the start of World War II, she is the only child her parents will have. Her father, an accomplished violinist in the Berlin Philharmonic Orchestra, finds little work in America, now mired in the Depression. Through a German friend, he secures a job as a music teacher in a public school in Erie. His spoken English is less than fluent, the books he reads are usually in German, and his school colleagues treat him with suspicion.

Pearl Harbor ends his dreams of a fruitful life in this country. He is taken away one night by military police and shipped with other "suspicious" German immigrants to an internment camp in North Carolina. Her mother, left destitute with a small child, makes an impassioned plea to government officials and is allowed to join him in the camp. She takes with them his violin, a ragdoll, and a single suitcase of clothes.

There they live for the duration of the war and beyond—in a barracks with coal stove, no running water, pubic latrines and mess halls, barbed wire fence and guard towers around the perimeter. She turns six, and though the war is over, they are kept on in the camp. One day, their single valuable possession, her father's violin, goes missing. Distraught, her father confronts a guard whom he suspects of the theft. A fight begins, and, in the presence of his horrified wife and daughter, the guard shoots him in the chest.

"My father's death felt like my death," she tells him in a trembling voice. "For nearly a year I didn't speak. I stared off into space in a kind of catatonic state. Because of my condition, my mother and I were released from the camp but threatened with deportation if we ever told the story of the camp or my father's death. I'm seventy-eight years old, and I've never uttered a word about it until now."

The story affects Max powerfully, viscerally—he feels a steel band tightening around his chest; it is difficult to breathe—yet he doesn't stop typing.

"I'd been lost in darkness for a long time. As we rode away from the camp in a military truck, sun began streaming through a side window. I touched my mother's arm and said, 'I'm hungry, Mama.' She burst into tears and pressed me to her neck. At the time I had no idea why she was acting in such a way.

"We returned by bus to Pennsylvania and discovered that our few possessions, entrusted to a friend, were gone. It was no surprise. The friend had moved back to what was left of Germany. My mother somehow found jobs cleaning churches. She took me along because there was no one to care for me. She was a strong woman. Her courage kept us alive. In time she married again—a good man, an American, who paid for my education. Life had been very bleak, and then suddenly, as if some kind of penance had been served, it brightened. I give thanks for it every day." She pauses, glancing away from Max, calming her emotions. "But forgive me. I'm getting ahead of my story."

Later, as they sit having their evening drink, Max says, "It's an incredible story, Mrs. Roloff."

"You're kind, Max." Obviously touched by his words, dropping her eyes, she strokes the stem of her sherry glass.

"Such awful, heartbreaking things. I can't imagine it."

"Yes, very dark things." She nods, staring into the amber liquid. "Do you see how it's a story that needs to be told? They can hardly deport me now, at my age. I just hope I can live to finish it."

They sit in silence. He is amazed at how much he feels for this old woman. It's six o'clock and dark outside, but the room is brightly lit. Unlike most old people, she is not frugal about electricity. She loves the light.

"We'll finish it," Max says to her with conviction. "We'll finish it."

CAT TALE

The cat wandered into Simon's life in the fall of the first pandemic year. It was a small, lithe female, black with intense grey-green eyes and a white, star-like shape on her chest. Simon rented a tiny, ground floor rear apartment with a covered porch overlooking an asphalt parking lot for eight units. The cat often huddled on the porch near his door or stretched out in the parking lot, which worried him. When he unloaded groceries and left the tailgate of his car open, she entered mysteriously without him noticing; he'd find her curled up in one of his passenger seats.

He was sure she lived in the neighborhood yet always seemed to be wandering and hungry. He bought a bag of cat treats and sometimes fed her. As the year neared November, the weather turned, but the cat was still hanging around outside most of the time, even at night. He found himself disturbed at owners so neglectful. Pets weren't allowed in the apartment house, but he began letting her in at night. He bought a small litter box and two small cat dishes. Though the one-bedroom apartment was tight, she found spots to sleep or to fold up and watch the world. She liked his wife's sewing table. It was at a window where she could stare out at birds and chatter quietly. When the weather grew wet and cold, she rarely went out. She spent time each day under the bed or sleeping against his wife's pillow. He watched for ads or signs about a lost cat but saw nothing.

Though she was not a lap cat, she was smart and clean and affectionate, slept at his feet at night and liked nuzzling his book while he was reading. Sometimes he called her Reading Cat, but he gave her a real name as well, Stella, for the star on her upper chest. Her slender, athletic build, her agility, reminded him of his wife, Celeste. The cat could leap to the top of a six-foot fence from a crouch.

Simon and Celeste had been married four years. Both of them had hospitality jobs in the city's largest hotel. Both had been furloughed when the pandemic had shut the place down. Five months into the crisis, they were terminated. Unemployment payments and stimulus checks kept them afloat, but their plans for a house of their own evaporated. Though Simon's nature leaned toward pessimism, Celeste was upbeat, undaunted. When he struggled with organizing his life, she quietly managed things. She'd been a gymnast in college, dark-haired, small, and amazingly nimble. She was nearly his only human contact during this strange, isolated time, but it was the happiest he'd ever been. Her positive energy charged him. She was skilled at sewing—set up a business in their apartment making designer cloth facemasks with an inside compartment for a disposable filter. She was clever at marketing online, her product was good, and within a short time she had more business than she could handle. He joined in— borrowed his mother's sewing machine and learned to sew masks, too.

Vaccines were still in development. One evening, several weeks before the cat appeared, Celeste became crushingly weary and went to bed with a fever. In the morning, he drove her to a med center where his fears were confirmed. She grew worse by midday. He rushed her to the downtown hospital, now impossibly overcrowded. She was wheeled away, but he wasn't allowed to go along. By the time a ventilator became available the following day, she was critical. Celeste was strong and thirty years old. He never got to see or speak with her before she died. No funeral gathering was possible, though both sets of parents drove from across state to be with him. As far as Simon was concerned, his life ended with hers.

He still slept on his side of the bed. His sleep was a leaden semi-consciousness, full of exhausting dreams—often searching for her in places, usually big cities, where they'd become hopelessly separated. A faint coconut smell of her shampoo lingered on her pillow. Her clothing lay untouched in her dresser and still hung in their shared closet. The orders for masks kept coming. On their website he posted delay notices, reassuring customers they would not be charged until the product was sent. He was not sure he could ever make another mask. They hadn't helped Celeste at all. Yet life refused to stop for his suffering. Her medical bills piled up. The rent still had to be paid.

The cat appeared a month after her death, and in his loneliness and despair he sensed a kindred lost spirit. She spent a lot of time on his porch.

A woman named Carly from the apartment above his began stopping every few days in those agonizing first weeks with small disposable aluminum casserole pans of food marked "For Simon." They'd never spoken more than a brief greeting before this, but she somehow knew about his loss. Most days, he looked like someone who slept under a viaduct. Carly always wore a mask when he saw her, so he wasn't even sure what she looked like. She seemed to live alone, though he wasn't certain of it. Her food was simple, well made, but he had little appetite, and the aluminum pans piled up in the refrigerator. He slipped a note under her door, thanking her, telling her the food was lovely.

Once the cat appeared, he noticed that Carly would kneel to speak to it when she came home from wherever she went. One day while she was rubbing the cat's neck, he opened his door and asked her in. She wore a mask; he didn't. An early snow was falling, and her spiky chestnut hair was full of snowflakes. She nodded, brushed by him as he held the door, and Stella slipped in behind her.

"Hey, that little cat just sneaked in," she said.

"It's okay. We have an arrangement. No one seems to be taking care of her, so I let her in when she wants and hope no one notices."

"Thank goodness! I was thinking about it myself. I feed her sometimes. So do a couple of the other tenants."

"Her owner ought to be horsewhipped."

Carly nodded agreement, shucked off her dark, quilted coat and dropped it on a chair. She wore jeans with torn knees, heavy work boots, large hoop earrings, and a sweatshirt with a 4H logo on it. "I look like crap," she said. "I'm mucking stalls at the stable where I board my horse. I lost my retail job, and it's all I can find that's halfway safe. Ten bucks an hour, but it's under the table so I still get un-employment."

"How can you afford a horse?"

"I can't. My parents pay the board, thank God. I'm struggling just to stay in this cheesy place."

Simon pulled out a chair for her and they both sat down at the kitchen table. "Want a beer?"

"Sure, if you don't mind me taking off my mask."

"Hell if I care. I don't worry much about it these days."

Carly pulled off her mask. Her small nose ring was a surprise. She was young, early twenties he guessed. She had a boyish, rough and tumble kind of cuteness that he'd seen before in some horse girls.

"Bet you were a barrel racer in 4H," he said, pulling open the refrigerator.

She spotted several of her weeks-old aluminum containers and laughed.

"Hey, sorry—your food is great," he said, embarrassed. "I just don't have much appetite right now. I thought only church ladies took food to people."

"My mom's a church lady. I help her out. This is my first solo run." She scratched the back of her head aggressively. "Yeah, I did some barrel racing. How'd you guess?"

"You have that look. I was in 4H when I was a kid. I wanted a horse, but my parents told me a rabbit was all they could afford.

English and Western Pleasure events weren't bad, but I loved barrel racing. There were some crazy riders."

She grinned. "Yeah, it helps to be crazy. I'd still do it, but my horse is getting too old."

He opened two bottles of beer. "Want a glass?"

She shook her head and drank from the bottle. He noticed Stella rubbing against her leg. Suddenly, the cat jumped on her lap.

"Wow, that's a first. She never does that."

Carly shrugged and smiled. "Probably because I smell like a barn." The cat curled up and stared at her. "She has the strangest eyes."

"Yeah, she's an odd little spirit. She's the one keeping me together right now."

Carly looked at him hard, her head slightly tilted. "How *are* you doing?"

"I'm okay, I guess."

"How could you be okay when you just lost your wife?"

He was startled and annoyed by her bluntness. The few people he ran into danced around the subject of Celeste. This one plowed in like a bulldozer. He sat a few moments without speaking. "I really appreciate the food, Carly, but your budget must be as tight as mine."

"Some things you don't worry about. Anyway, I just give you half of what I make for myself. No big deal."

"Well...thanks."

"Are you talking to anybody?"

"Talking? What do you mean?"

"Jeez...what do you think, Simon? Can I call you Simon? You don't even know me, I realize, but I'm willing to listen. Believe me, you gotta talk to someone about it."

He took a long swallow of beer. "Maybe some time." He couldn't imagine sharing anything remotely personal with her.

"Good. Just knock on my door." She finished her beer, nudged the cat off her lap, and stood to leave. "Thanks for taking care of this little critter. I'm relieved someone's doing it, and I won't tell the landlord."

"I named her Stella."

"For that little white star, I bet. I like it. I'll be seeing you."

She shut his door and went up the stairs, leaving a void behind her. Her brash presumptuousness had unsettled his isolation, but at the same time it was a relief to have even a tenuous connection with someone besides a cat. That night, Stella slept against his wife's pillow instead of at his feet. His dreams changed, softened, and he slept better. He had a vivid sense that he was lying in Celeste's arms, and when he awoke refreshed, he felt he'd made love to her, so real was the illusion. The cat still slept peacefully against her pillow.

That morning, he showered, shaved, and got dressed in something other than sweats. In the living room he found a roll of cotton flannel draped from the sewing table. Stella had apparently gotten playful and batted the roll to the floor. He stared at the orange material and, absurd as it was, sensed the cat was telling him something to the effect of "Get it in gear, Simon." That day he cut and sewed (inner layer of flannel, outer layer of quilter's cotton) a small stack of masks against back-logged orders of several hundred. By dinnertime he discovered he hadn't eaten all day, stopped and slipped a frozen pizza into the oven, tossed out Carly's aluminum pans, and opened a beer.

He guessed he had made twelve masks. Celeste had been able to do twice that number in the same period of time. Yet the next morning when he counted them, he found eighteen masks. He was pleased with himself and surprised.

Late the next day, he was still cutting material when a sharp knock startled him back to an awareness of the room he was in. He hurried to the door, figuring it could only be Carly. Instead, he found Ralph, his landlord, standing with his hands in the pockets of his bib overalls. Ralph was a burly, white-bearded man of about sixty, a handyman who took good care of his apartment building. Ralph had never come to his door before, so Simon was startled, and then instantly afraid the cat might be nearby and visible.

"Hi, Simon," Ralph said mildly.

"Hi, Ralph. What's up?"

"Well, yesterday I was fixing a storm door, and I noticed a cat sitting in your window. You know I don't allow pets in the house. You'll need to find another place for it."

Simon silently cursed his carelessness. "It's not my cat," he said. "It belongs to some neighbor, but they don't take care of it. I'm just keeping it alive through the worst of the winter."

"Yeah, I've seen it hanging around. I feel bad for the poor thing, but if I let you do it, I'll have other tenants wanting the same privileges. Sorry, Simon."

Simon felt his heart slump. "Yeah—me, too. I'll just have to find some kind of place for her. Maybe my parents will take her." He knew he wasn't about to haul the poor creature across the state to a condo that charged a fee for pets.

"I'll give you till the end of the week," Ralph said.

That evening Simon paid Carly a visit. An add-on exterior stairway, disfiguring the back of the old Victorian house, led to a small upper deck, her apartment and two others. She opened to his knock, dressed in a sweatshirt and flannel pajama bottoms.

"Hi, Simon. What's happening?" She led him inside and gestured toward a worn leather chair. Nearby it hung a Western saddle on a metal rack and beside that a small bookcase crammed with books; on top stood a neat row of barrel racing trophies. The walls were hung with masterly drawings of horses, some framed and others not, several with large Best of Show ribbons attached to the frames. The place was spare, simple, neatly kept. "So, you want to talk now?"

His eyes left the drawings. "No, I'm here for something else. Ralph found out about Stella today. He saw her sitting in the window, and he won't bend the rules." He sank into the sagging cushion.

"Hell, just bring her up here," she said without hesitation. "Ralph can't see in my windows, and he never comes in without letting me know."

Simon exhaled heavily. "That's terrific, Carly. I'm relieved."

"I'll show you where I keep my extra key. Come in to see her any time you want."

"Honestly?"

"Knock first if you think I'm here. Now and then my boyfriend stops by."

"Tell me something. Are these your drawings?"

"Well, sure."

"They're amazing."

"Come on, Simon, don't get carried away."

He shrugged, not feeling as though he was in the least carried away. He made his way downstairs with a new, less definite sense of her.

And so the problem was solved, at least temporarily, and Stella seemed to have little apprehension about changing homes. Carly proved every bit as acceptable to her as Simon was, and her apartment was larger by one small room used for storage. The litter box and food went in there.

The winter came and dragged its way along. The cat now stayed in all the time. Simon dreaded Christmas without Celeste. Carly, apparently sensing it, tried to raise his spirits by cutting a Christmas tree. He helped her haul it up the back stairs and set it up. Doing his best to sound upbeat, he drew attention again to her horse drawings.

"I like to draw animals, horses especially," she said off-handedly. "I've done it since I was a kid."

"Who taught you?"

"Nobody, Simon, I taught myself. I took an art class at community college once, but I didn't learn much I didn't already know."

She handed him a sketch pad with a dozen rough drawings of Stella in various postures and moods. As he looked through it, he was stunned at how accurately she'd captured the enigmatic nature, the exotic curvature of the cat. "Amazing," was all he could think to say.

The real cat lay curled up under the bare Christmas tree like a present wrapped in black. The glossy look of her made him think of his wife's dark hair, her soft inner glow.

On Christmas Eve Carly went off to a late church service; she asked him along but he declined. On Christmas morning he stayed in bed in the dim light of a slate-gray sky, with no signs around him of the season. Both sets of parents called to wish him a merry Christmas, and he lied to them about his state of mind. He opened the single present—from his parents—a black sweater that he pulled on over his tee shirt. The sweater was tight. He'd let himself go—done no exercise since a last long hike on the beach with Celeste.

That afternoon he noticed a Ram pickup truck in the driveway, parked in an absent tenant's space—Carly's boyfriend, no doubt, spending the holiday with her. Simon longed for the comfort of the black cat but didn't dare intrude on them.

The following day, Carly invited him up and gave him a bottle of wine as a belated Christmas gift. At his urging, she uncorked the bottle, they toasted and drank, and after a second glass, she began asking him a few cautious questions about Celeste. Stella purred loudly and rubbed her muzzle against his legs. Warmed by the wine but especially the cat, he surprised himself by opening up a little: Celeste, he told her, loved interesting foods but didn't like to cook; she was a Pied Piper for children, but never spoke of having them; she loved books, read long after he was asleep each night; she woke up happy and stayed that way, a light in his frequent dark moods, though her childhood had been marred by an alcoholic father. Talking seemed to help unknot something in him and further assure him she was, in some mysterious way, still watching over him.

Early in the new year people his age became eligible for the vaccine, and he stood in line to get it. Feeling safer and faintly more social now, Simon accepted Carly's invitation to meet her boyfriend Randy, a farrier who drove the covered Ram pickup with pullout shelves of horseshoes. Simon had spoken to him in passing, but they'd never really talked. Randy was in his late twenties, about Simon's age—yet already complaining of a farrier's bad back. He did some bull-riding in rodeos, which didn't help any. The Western hat he wore made him look bigger than he was. He was rougher-edged than Carly, friendly enough but outspoken about mistrusting vaccines and facemasks. He declared he wasn't about to let anyone, especially the government, tell him what to do. Simon didn't mention his online facemask business, but he was wearing one of them. Randy said he had no beef about masks as long as everyone had a free choice.

Later, after Randy had left, Carly came down to Simon's apartment for a beer. "Sometimes I'm not sure why I go with him," she told him. "He's a nice guy at heart, and he looks kind of like Jake Owen to me, but he's pretty set in his thinking. He spends a lot of time on social media—that's part of the trouble. Randy is real good with horses, though. He talks soft to the ones who don't want their feet worked on, and they settle down. I love that. It's the main thing about him that attracted me. He's the kind of guy I always figured I'd end up with. He has a way with horses."

"How is he with cats?"

She shrugged. "The first thing he did was step on Stella's tail. She was lying under the chair, and he didn't see her."

"Supposed to be bad luck."

"Hell, Randy makes his own bad luck. That little cat feels like good luck to me."

Simon smiled. "Yeah, she does."

Carly wandered around the room, sipping her beer. She looked over the sewing machine and then picked up a finished mask lying in a stack. "So this is how you make a living?"

"Yeah. My wife started an online business, and I'm struggling to keep it going. You need an extra job? I've got four hundred orders to fill and more coming in every day. I can't catch up."

"How much would I make?"

"Depends on how much you work."

"What if I did it full time?"

Simon shrugged. "I'd give you the profits on everything you make. We'd share the mailing part of it, which I hate."

It took her about five minutes to figure out she'd do much better than her present salary. Her unemployment was about to end, so in the next two minutes they formed a partnership with a handshake and another beer. A weight fell from his shoulders. She surprised him, adjusting to change so nonchalantly. She mentioned that they'd better make masks as fast as they could because the pandemic wasn't going to last forever. That obvious detail had somehow never occurred to him.

They moved a sewing machine upstairs to the kitchen of her slightly roomier apartment. Within a week, Carly, wearing one of her Western riding shirts, had an inspiration as she was staring at the rhinestone jewels on her shirt cuffs. She began sewing the jewels on masks, and a new, more exclusive line was born. Orders arrived daily, but they managed to make gains in output. Two worked better than one, and their production grew apace. The numbers they managed as a team sometimes confounded them both.

Simon was often in Carly's apartment because of the cat. Stella contentedly wandered from Carly's lap (why only *her* lap?) to Simon's legs, rubbing against them till he reached down and scratched her back. They did all the packaging and mailing there and sometimes ate together. She was faster and more efficient at everything than he was (which rankled him a bit, as it sometimes had with Celeste). They settled on splitting profits instead of counting what each had done. More than once, Carly marveled at how many masks they'd made— more than either of them expected.

When they worked together, she usually was braless in old tee shirts, not intending to be sexy, he could tell, but just being who she was. His sexual thoughts were all about Celeste anyway. How had he ever thought that the aura of a beloved wife faded at death? He found it comforting and oddly unsettling that he felt her presence in small ways nearly every day. At times, he wondered if he was entirely sane.

On a day the two of them were working upstairs packing up mailers, Carly put a pot roast in the oven, and the longer it cooked, the more delectable the aroma became.

"Hey," he said. "I have a bottle of Merlot in my apartment. If I can stay for dinner, I'll share the bottle with you. That pot roast smells like heaven."

"Well, sure, Simon. I planned to ask you anyway. Don't tell Randy, though. He's getting kind of strange about us being together so much."

"What is *that* all about?" Simon was sincerely puzzled.

That evening she moved the sewing machine and put candles on the table; they ate the feast in near-silent pleasure, the cat curled at their feet. Then, seemingly out of nowhere, Carly asked, "What is marriage like, Simon? Is it worth it?"

"Damn, Carly, what a question." He thought for a while before answering. "Yeah, it's worth it. I got lucky, though. Celeste was like warm sunshine every day. She was the center of my life, but the trouble is now there's no center. Maybe some things are just too good to lose. I can't seem to get past it."

She looked intently at him. "You two worked at the same place, didn't you?"

"Yeah, a hotel job I didn't like, one she talked me into taking, but with her beside me, it didn't matter. My degree is in journalism—a dying profession. Couldn't find a job."

She drank some wine, staring into the glass. "So, what did you two do for fun?"

He shrugged, puzzled at her direction. He glanced at the floor where Stella sat staring at him with those inscrutable eyes. "A lot of things. Worked out together. She was a nut for it. We hiked trails. We sat in the woods and watched birds. We played guitars together. We drank wine and talked for hours about everything you can think of. She was smart about people. I was a better person just hanging around her."

Carly's look got more serious. "Was sex a big part of it?"

He could feel a flush run up his neck. "How the hell am I supposed to answer that?"

She wasn't embarrassed. "I just wondered. It seems to be a major deal for guys. At least the ones I know."

"Yeah, it was important. But in a very natural way, like the talking we did. Just another lovely way we connected."

She smiled. "That's what I hoped you'd say. I'm asking because, well, Randy and I just got engaged."

He took a moment to absorb that, and then looked down at his plate where one carrot swam in a puddle of gravy. "Honestly?"

She hesitated. "Do you think I'm making a mistake?"

He took a deep breath. "How old are you?"

"Almost twenty-two."

"I'd say wait a little. Randy seems to have some settling down to do."

"Yeah, but what if I lose him in the process?"

He finished off his glass of wine in a swallow. "You're just a kid. It wouldn't be the end of the world."

"So you say. But I'm not exactly a great catch."

"Jeez, Carly, give yourself some credit." He saw beneath the tough exterior some insecurity he'd never noticed. Just then the cat jumped up on Carly's lap and stretched out with a sigh. "Do you love the guy?"

"I think I do. I guess I'm still trying to figure that out."

"Well…do you have a date set?"

"Nope. He isn't ready. He's still trying to get his business going. I don't even have a ring."

"Good. Just take your time."

"I was thinking September."

"*Take your time*. Find something you're sure about." He wasn't at all clear about why he was feeling protective of her.

"Sure about?" She smiled at him. "Well anyway, thanks, Simon. I appreciate your advice even if I don't end up taking it."

They both laughed and finished off the bottle of Merlot, the cat dozing on her lap.

Late that night, Simon awoke to a familiar sound. Someone was working at the sewing machine, lit only by moonlight through the nearby window.

"Carly?" he asked.

Whoever it was didn't turn but kept on sewing. He sat up in bed. "Who's there?"

She turned her head, and he saw—with surprising clarity in the half-light—his wife Celeste. Her presence caused him no alarm. He felt, in fact, abnormally calm.

"Celeste, is it you?"

She turned to face him, smiled, and went back to her sewing.

"What are you doing here?"

She didn't answer, but went on serenely with her work.

"I've felt you around, but I didn't think—"

A light knock on the door jarred him. His bedside clock read 3:10 a.m. He jumped out of bed, rushed through the kitchen and opened to Carly. Her hair was disheveled, her look a bit wild. She wore a rodeo sweatshirt and flannel shorts.

"Is Stella down here?" she whispered loudly. "I can't find her anywhere."

Simon took her arm and pulled her inside. He pointed to the sewing table. "I have a visitor," he said.

"Where?" Her look was bewildered. No one sat at the sewing table. Celeste was gone.

Simon slumped onto the couch.

"The cat isn't here?" she asked again.

"No."

"Are you okay, Simon?"

"No. But let's go search your place. She has to be hiding somewhere."

They went upstairs, and, sure enough, they found her hidden under the saddle rack, a place she'd never gone before. He sat down on Carly's bed, and she made them both a mug of tea. Stella jumped up on the sewing table and stared at them.

Simon massaged the back of his neck. "Know how we've wondered about getting so many masks done in a day?" he asked. "Well, tonight I found out there's someone helping us." He hesitated. "I woke up and saw a woman working at my sewing table, and I wasn't dreaming. She looked right at me, smiled, but never spoke."

"That's weird. Who was it?"

He took a deep breath. "My wife. She's making masks for us while we sleep."

She stared at him, sat down on the bed, and took a slow sip of tea. "Your dead wife? Jeez, Simon, did that Merlot get to you?"

"She must like your rhinestone idea. She was sewing them on when I saw her."

"You're freaking me out, Simon."

"Yeah, I'm freaking myself out, too. I'm just telling you what I saw. She was sewing masks for us."

"But why?"

"I guess she thought we could use the help."

Stella chose that moment to jump down from the sewing table, then up onto the bed and settle between them, purring loudly. Carly absently scratched behind her ears.

The following night, Randy showed up at Carly's place. Simon noticed him park his rig in one of the tenant's spots, directly in front of a sign saying unauthorized vehicles would be towed. In fact, the cockeyed angle he parked took up two spaces. Randy had done it before—he generally ignored rules.

Simon guessed from the stiff, dignified way he climbed the stairs he'd come from a bar. Uneasy, Simon saw Carly let him in, returned to the television set where a spring training baseball game was just starting. During the second inning he heard loud voices from Carly's place. He got up to look. After a few moments, the noise settled down, but he was genuinely worried. He kept going to his kitchen window and glancing up the stairs. At the end of the third inning, he heard the whine of a truck. He looked out to see a squat, greasy man raising Randy's rig and then towing it away. He also saw his landlord Ralph standing in the driveway observing the drama. Simon stepped out onto his porch.

At that moment, Randy came roaring down the steps and straight up to Ralph, nose to nose. Ralph didn't flinch.

"What the hell are you doing with my rig?"

Ralph pointed calmly to the sign. "Can't you read, son?"

"Dammit, I wasn't going to stay long. Why'd you do it?"

"Got a complaint from a tenant. You're in her space."

"*Who* complained?" Randy's face began turning puce.

Carly showed up next, looking palc and upset. Simon moved off the porch to get nearer to her.

"Woman in apartment two."

"That's my apartment," Simon said.

"Yeah, it was your wife. I know her voice." Ralph hesitated. "Oh, wait, that can't be it, can it. Sorry, Simon. It slipped my mind. I don't know who it was."

Randy cursed hotly and ordered Carly to drive him to the impound lot.

"Take a cab," she spat back at him. She tossed Simon a dagger-like look, and slammed back up the stairs.

"I'll drive you," Simon said, bewildered.

Randy grumbled and cursed but followed him to the car.

The impound lot was out in a field on the edge of town, with a prison-like chain link fence barring entrance. It cost Randy $180 to get his truck out of impoundment. While Simon sat with him waiting for paperwork to be finished, Randy told him in a low growl, "That's the end of it."

"The end of what?"

"Carly and me." He laughed sharply. "As if you didn't know. I got no inclination to get tied down anyhow. She wants kids and a nice little farm to keep horses. Not what I'm dreaming about, believe me. She's all yours, Simon."

Simon sat befuddled. "Hell, Randy, she's not mine. We run a business together and nothing else. Where'd you get such a crazy idea?"

"Give me a break, man," Randy said with a snort. "You think I'm an idiot?"

Simon did, but he had the grace not to say it.

When Simon got back to his apartment, the ballgame was ending, and moments later Carly came bursting in, looking distraught. He offered her a beer, but she didn't want it.

"She's trying to break Randy and me up," she said, sounding miserable.

"Who is?"

"Your wife, who do you think?"

"That's absolutely crazy."

"No, it's not."

"Why would she do that?"

"I'm trying to figure it out. I have a funny feeling that little black cat is in on it, too."

Simon denied all of it, though certain of her speculations made him wonder.

Carly tried for several weeks to patch things up with Randy, but nothing worked. She went through a long, irksome period of mourning and then was okay again. The cat lived on, a small shadowy spirit, in her apartment.

Celeste appeared to Simon one more time, and this time she spoke. It was a March night of heavy storms. He was worried about Stella who scrambled under a bed at the first distant rumble of thunder. He was sitting on the couch reading, thinking about phoning Carly to see how the cat was, and glanced up just as lightning flashed. At the window he saw Celeste. She stood, hands folded in front of her, watching him.

"Hello, Celeste," he said.

She nodded.

Of all the things he might say, this peculiar question came out, "Why in the world did you call Ralph?"

She smiled her most radiant, loving smile—so beautiful it caused him pain. "You know she's too good for the cowboy."

"What does that matter to you?"

"Your well-being matters to me, Simon."

Lightning flashed in the window behind her, his eyes moved to the light, and when they shifted back, she was gone.

Simon and Carly remained together as business partners and did well for another year and a half until the pandemic began to wind down. Simon, for reasons he didn't fully understand (mutual love of the cat aside), was reluctant to end the association, so he proposed an idea that intrigued her.

Together, he suggested, they would write and illustrate a children's book. They would name it *Magic Stella*—a story about a shape-shifting good witch named Stella, who lived in a tumbledown house deep in the woods and who traveled about the countryside as a black cat, fixing lives in magical ways.

Together, they made a story of it, one both of them felt they knew: the people who fed the black cat and gave her shelter tended to be the poorer ones. The kindest of all of these, a young widow with two small children, baked bread through most of each night to sell the following day. One morning, though, exhausted from long hours without rest, she woke in horror knowing she'd made no bread. That meant no bread for customers, no money, no food for her children. Yet on the hearth where the black cat lay sleeping, she discovered a dozen large loaves already risen and ready to bake. Stella opened her mysterious eyes, fixing them on the young widow, who reached and stroked her gently.

Stella stayed with the young widow and her family a year; the bread became well known for excellence, and the young widow's business flourished, as did her children. She was able to hire an assistant and to buy a horse and delivery wagon from a kind blacksmith, who began stopping evenings to visit her. On the day after a year had passed, the black cat vanished from the young widow's house, never to be seen again in that part of the countryside.

Simon and Carly needed eight very lean months to get the book written, illustrated, and published and four more to find an audience. But suddenly it sold, and other *Magic Stella* books followed, praised particularly for their remarkable art and vivid, unusual characters. The pair continued working together (if now and then contentiously) for three more productive years, at which point they bowed at last to what seemed curiously inevitable: out of the fertile soil of creative symbiosis and mutual respect, one inch at a time, love had grown. They married in a simple ceremony, a cat and two friends as witnesses.

Though Simon never saw his beloved Celeste again, some sense of her always remained. Stella, their cat for life (featured in several magazine articles set at their small farm), was given the run of both barn and house to continue her enigmatic ways.

FAMILY SLIDES

It's dark and dream-like as I stare at my family on the beige, water-stained paneling of my parents' basement wall. It's mid-summer, but the space is cool and damp as a cave. Carousel projectors haven't been manufactured for years, but this one miraculously still works. I control the slide advance with a button on the machine. Surprisingly clear and sharp after fifty years in a moldering cardboard box, the slides give me a glimpse of a lost world, a shadowy past causing me unexpected emotional stress. At moments I laugh out loud, moan quietly, or whimper and shake my head. I'm thankful I'm alone.

My mother, now long dead, is in many of the shots because my father usually takes them. Though a mother of two, she isn't even marginally maternal. I once heard a neighbor call her a prima donna. She does a little acting locally. My father handles most of the cooking, takes us to the park, teaches us to ride bikes, reads to us at night. She has no interest in doing the work of filling photo albums, so she and my father have nearly all our family photographs developed in slide format. She does take the time to fit the small squares into empty carousels. I remember watching them once and never seeing them again.

The carousel box is labeled in her handwriting: "Christmas, 1973." I'm startled immediately by the image of my mother toasting the camera with a glass of red wine. She is glamorous in an overblown way, her hair in a beehive, her lipstick too pink, her lashes too long and black. Aging is her enemy. She wears a tight dress printed with large pink roses. Her smile is bright and posed. In the background I see my older sister Kitty (my mother calls her Princess, yet seems to discover her only when boys start lining up at the door), walking through with a small suitcase. She is leaving, if I remember rightly, to spend the holidays with her latest boyfriend at his family's house on Lake Geneva. His parents are relatives of the Wrigleys. My mother adores him, especially his wealth.

I touch the button and John Russell Owens III appears, standing beside Kitty just inside our front door. He is impressive in a camel topcoat—a handsome young banker-to-be who races sailboats and plays excellent tennis. He has seen her in a local production of *HMS Pinafore*. Her voice is lovely. Kitty will soon marry him, have two children, become an alcoholic, and go through a divorce after eight years of emotional abuse. The settlement is generous, but she is granted only limited custody of the children and remains an alcoholic.

I groan audibly and hit the button: my father and I are decorating the Christmas tree. He is in his early forties here, though over ninety now and his mind starting to fail. Not long ago I reluctantly moved him to a nursing facility. My sister, presently in rehab again, is unavailable to help. With some hired college muscle, I'm clearing out my parents' house—seventy years of accretion—yet if I don't stop the nostalgic side trips, the place will never be ready to sell. I'm searching for something, I guess, a clue to a mystery clouding my life.

I stare at the image of my young self. I'm in my freshman year of college and home for just the first time. I'm putting our old glass angel on the top of the tree. My hair is shoulder length, my jeans wide bellbottoms with a peace sign on a back pocket. Kent State has already happened. The war in Vietnam is nearly over. I missed being drafted, thank God, but my hair and outfit express my disenchantment with the country.

My father has the tree lights up, I see, and has started with decorations. He is hooking on a red apple ornament near the top of the tree. He looks pleased. The apple ornament causes me anxiety, though I'm not sure why. The two of us are the Christmas fanatics of the family. Together, we cut the tree and decorate inside and out. My mother finds our extravagance quite trashy. She puts up with us but doesn't participate. She likes my father's positive spirit but considers him a failure. He has a route delivering milk and dairy products. She's embarrassed to tell people what he does for a living.

I press the button, and a new image appears. Now my father is grinning at the camera, draping handfuls of silver tinsel on the branches…tons too much. The tree looks smothered, but for some reason he loves the effect. I disagree with him but don't complain because his enthusiasm is so infectious.

The next image amuses me. I'm standing beside my first car, an aging VW Beetle. My look is serious, my long hair newly cut for job purposes. I'm wearing a mail carrier's vest over my winter coat with a mailbag slung over my shoulder—a temporary employee of the U.S. Government, a young man of flexible principles.

That time comes back in a rush, as do memories of an unusual woman and a demented dog.

With a scholarship and part-time work, I'm managing to pay my way through college—in this case as a substitute mail carrier through nearly three weeks of the holiday season. In the summers I'm a bellhop at a downtown hotel. My parents help me when they can, but on one salary (my mother volunteers but doesn't work), they are hard pressed to meet their own expenses. My sister has finished hair styling school after trying college, is employed at a local salon and doing my mother's hair and nails at no cost in our kitchen. Those two seem a matched pair. Are my father and I? I've never been sure.

I stare at the image as if in a trance. I can hardly remember being that young.

The job's dull routine comes back like a jerky super 8 film playing in my head: sort mail in the morning in the stuffy downtown main office and walk the mail route all afternoon. Snow falls nearly every day—heavy, sloppy snow with packed ice underneath. My route is in one of the oldest, shabbiest parts of town, down near the river, the residents primarily Polish and black. I start on Lafayette Street walking a flat plane beside the river. That's the easy part. Most of my mail customers are on perpendicular streets running up the bluff. Three of those streets are cobblestone—difficult to drive but worse to walk, yet I have to cross them multiple times. Few people shovel their sidewalks. Plows have difficulty with the steep incline and cobbled road surfaces. I manage to fall three times in my first day of delivering.

Within a few days, I begin to get the hang of staying upright, but I have problems yet to face. I see myself walking the shoveled path to a yellow mailbox beside the front door of a neat white house with two strips of concrete for a driveway. I hold a handful of what are obviously Christmas cards destined for the yellow mailbox. Whoever lives here has friends. Christmas cards aren't a big part of most of my route. Government checks and food stamp cards are far more common—people come outside in the cold to wait for them, and when they don't arrive, the mail carrier, a flunky of an uncaring federal government, suffers their wrath. I tell them I'm just a sub, but they curse me anyway.

I'm reaching for the yellow mailbox when I hear pounding paws, a savage, terrifying growl. I turn and the mail in my hand goes flying. A black dog with graying hair on his face has clamped my left forearm in his jaws. I feel pressure but no tearing of flesh. The guttural sounds coming out of him are strange. I try to pull away and the sleeve of my thick winter coat rips at the shoulder seam. The front door opens and a black woman appears. She rushes out on the porch in a housedress and apron and shouts at the dog.

"Chen! Get your black ass down!" She points a finger and stares hard at him. He lets go of me and sits, looking cowed and guilty. A broken rope hangs from his collar. She bends and picks it up.

"You go inside. I'll be right back. My neighbor keeps him tied all the time. Poor dog breaks the rope. He's old and can't bite hard.

But he's the reason the mailbox is out by the front fence. Post Office wouldn't deliver otherwise. Go in now. I'll fix that sleeve."

"Your mail went everywhere. Sorry." I bend and begin picking it up.

"No problem, honey. You get inside and sit down. I'll have you back on the job in no time."

So I go inside the white house. Though I'm shaken, the place feels warm and welcoming, with a decorated Christmas tree in the living room beside a sofa. She has a fire going in a fireplace across the room. I can smell something sweet baking in the oven. She returns in half a minute and helps me out of my coat.

"I'm Mrs. Lawrence."

"I'm Micah."

"I do like those Bible names." She sits and opens a sewing box, finds the right color thread and begins sewing up the sleeve. "Haven't seen you delivering before."

"I'm subbing through the holidays. I'm in college."

She smiles, and I notice how open and pretty her face is. Her skin is a soft brown and her eyes a darker shade of brown. "My son's at University of Detroit. He'll be here for Christmas."

"That's great," I say, relaxing into her friendliness. "I'm at MSU."

"Good for you, Micah. Bet your folks are proud."

There's a light rap on her front door. "That's my milkman. Would you mind letting him in?"

I go to the door and open, shocked for a moment to see my father standing on the porch dressed in his white Buttercup Dairy uniform and jaunty milkman's hat, holding his metal carrier of bottles, cheeses, and butter. He stares at me with his mouth open wide.

"Micah. What in heavens are you doing here?"

Mrs. Lawrence answers for me. "Mr. Zhang's dog ripped the sleeve off his coat. I'm fixing it. You two know each other?"

My father's astonishment softens into a smile. "He's my son."

She looks up from her sewing with a sparkle in her eyes. "Well, imagine that. Both of you sit down at the table. There's something nice in the oven I'd like you to try. Two quarts of milk, half pound of butter, wedge of sharp cheddar today, Tom."

'I have a nice baby Swiss, Ruth, if you're interested."

She smiles at him and nods. Their easy use of first names is curious to me, though her embracing nature invites it. They have a friendly connection, it's clear. My father goes to her small refrigerator and puts her order on a shelf. He sets down his metal carrier and meanders over to her Christmas tree.

"Now this is beautiful," he says. "Micah and I put a tree up a few days ago." He touches an ornament, a red apple that looks just like ours. "I like this especially."

She laughs softly and says "Forbidden fruit. Yeah, it's my favorite."

She finishes my coat and takes a tray of cinnamon rolls from the oven, puts them on a plate, and bastes them with white icing. We all sit at the kitchen table, she pours coffee, and we eat. The rolls are so incredibly good that my puzzled thoughts about her "forbidden fruit" remark vanish. Surprisingly, so does my growing dislike of my job. The sugar and cinnamon act like some magic drug that sweetens the day for me. I feel just the way I'd like life always to feel. I reluctantly leave to finish my route. My father stays on to have another cinnamon roll.

Later, when I've three times seen his truck at her house for longer than normal delivery time, I ask him about her. He's happy to tell me. Ruth Lawrence is a good friend—a widow who works as a waitress at night. She supports her son in college and struggles to make ends meet, though she never complains. She has no car—takes buses, even late at night. As for her cinnamon rolls, she somehow mixes love into them in mysterious ways.

I think of my mother, who has use of our Mercury every day because my father drives a company truck. She belongs to a bridge club, a drama club, a dance club, and it doesn't take a genius to see the difference in the two women. My father, aglow now, tells me, "The lady is pure sunshine. She's the only one who can warm up that hermit neighbor of hers—takes him a plate of her cinnamon rolls and a biscuit for the dog."

My father's admiration for some reason depresses me.

The Christmas carousel has come full circle. I lift it from the base and replace it with another that reads "Kitty's Wedding, 1974." I vividly recall disliking everything about the occasion except for a few moments of the church ceremony. The reception, held at a posh local country club, becomes an uncomfortable division of haves and have nots. Though the Owens (cool to their son's choice of partners) offer to pay for more than just the alcohol, my father refuses and ends up spending miles beyond his means. My mother and Kitty contribute to his financial woes, hoping to impress the Owens, which of course they don't. The first frame shows Kitty holding up her absurdly expensive wedding dress. I can't bring myself to go through the agony of seeing this all again, so I put the wedding carousel back in the box and find another, labeled "Kitty and Family."

I now gaze at slides I've never seen before: a shot of the palatial Owens house on Lake Geneva. Next, I see a hugely pregnant Kitty, sitting with my mother and John Russell Owens III in the Owens' gleaming mahogany Chris-Craft launch, cruising the lake. My mother looks supremely happy—much happier than Kitty.

I'm in none of these slides. I don't see my father, either, though he may be the photographer. It must be mid to later 1970s, and I'm in grad school out of state. I see a shot of John and Kitty's impressive first house in Oak Park with a BMW in the driveway and a tennis court at the side. Kitty sits on the porch. My mother holds a baby, Jillian. A maid is serving coffee. I hit the button quickly, dismayed.

I see an image of my mother behind a slick-haired, ruggedly handsome young man on a motorcycle. I exhale heavily. Her arms are around him, her body tight to his back. I study them a minute—he's half her age. My father surely isn't the photographer here. I shake my head and go on. I see the young man in the next slide, leaning out of the window of a limousine. I remember now—he's Reggie, the Owens' chauffeur. Whenever my parents are invited to a Lake Geneva gathering, he drives an hour to pick them up and takes them back afterwards. My father goes only once and makes excuses thereafter. My mother relishes every moment of every trip.

I see an image of Kitty sitting on her porch, pregnant again, looking worn at the edges. My mother stands beside her, radiant and pleased. Her look says, "This is life as it is meant to be." Jillian stands in a playpen nearby with a pacifier in her mouth.

I realize no one is compelling me to watch this mounting disaster. I stop and change carousels to one that is labeled simply "1982." For our family, it's a highly memorable year, though this particular carousel, the last one in the box, contains only a few slides.

The two most significant 1982 dates are these: early February, 1982—my sister's marriage ends in acrimonious divorce. Two young children are left in limbo. June 9, 1982—my mother's life ends behind the wheel of the Mercury in our closed garage with the engine running. She's forty-eight. I'm the one who finds her. I have agonizing dreams about that experience many times over the years, always half wondering if cinnamon rolls and forbidden fruit are somehow involved. Yet no one is certain it is a suicide. My mother is brash but not brave. There are limits to her dramatics. Just before she goes to the garage, she drains a bottle of Southern Comfort…starts the car and maybe passes out…it's possible. At the time she is obviously in some sort of massive pain. I suspect I'll never know the source.

My father, after the funeral, can't bear to drive the Mercury, trades it to a dealer for a used Chevy. My family, throughout most of the remaining year, is in ruins.

It's with real apprehension that I touch the carousel button. The image that appears is of a man I don't immediately recognize. He sits at our kitchen table looking down at papers spread in front of him. He's dapper, middle-aged, graying at the temples. His pinstriped suit looks Italian and expensive. In the next slide he is standing at our front door. My mother is holding his arm. I suddenly remember. It's David O'Conner, Kitty's divorce lawyer. What is he doing with my mother? Who took the photo? In the following shot he is standing beside a black Mercedes in our driveway.

I remember the black Mercedes from another time: I'm teaching English in a nearby suburban high school, living in an apartment. I need a book from home so I drop in unexpectedly. I see the Mercedes parked across the street. I still have a key, so I let myself in and call out to my mother. I hear some quiet scurrying upstairs. She appears a few minutes later in a robe.

"Micah, what a nice surprise," she tells me, smiling brightly. She says she's been in the shower, though her hair isn't wet.

She gathers herself, has me sit at the kitchen table and pours coffee. I tell her the reason I'm there, and she follows with a dozen aimless questions about my teaching. I glance out the kitchen window as she yammers, and I notice the Mercedes disappearing down the street. Later, when I ask Kitty about David O'Conner, she tells me he has moved to the firm's San Francisco office.

I press the button once more, half expecting images of funeral flowers in the church sanctuary or of people gathering afterwards at the house, but the projector bulb squeals weirdly, sputters, and loudly pops—ending, blessedly, the overlong life of this poor machine. I sit in darkness, shaken and short of breath.

My father dies before I'm able to get the house cleared and sold. Ruth Lawrence has been dead only a few years. The two never marry—I'm not sure why. After my mother's death, when a decent period has passed, my father begins going to Ruth's house nearly every day, frequently staying the night. She rarely comes to our house, though neither Kitty nor I live there. He drives her to work and picks her up. They shop for groceries, share expenses, enjoy her cinnamon rolls, go out occasionally to movies. Both cook well, eat together every night, and clearly make each other happy, yet when in her early seventies her son asks her to move to upper New York to live with his wife and him, she does it. My father grows very old after that. He travels once to see her, but that's all.

I inherit the house, since Kitty doesn't want it, and at this point I've all but decided to move in. It's a good house.

There have been several women in my life, but I've never married. As a result, there are no children or grandchildren coming to visit. It's pleasantly uncomplicated. I rarely see Kitty's grownup kids. I cut and decorate a tree every Christmas. I am a year or two past retirement age yet still teaching—and I suspect I'll continue till they carry me out. I have some good friends—fellow teachers and a procession of students whom I run into in the most unexpected places. I've traveled a lot. I've written several books of stories, trying to make sense of life.

It remains indecipherable.

EYE OF THE PEACOCK

Harold Flowers went to City Park nearly every day to eat and to avoid the lunchroom conversations of his fellow New Vision seminarians, especially their bean-counting claims about people they'd led to Christ. They reminded him of life insurance salesmen closing deals. It didn't help that Harold was older than most of them, a late starter in this world of God-seeking.

He didn't like evangelizing, especially in the heavy-handed ways of these young enthusiasts. But he knew he somehow had to learn to do it (but not as they did)—such was the Great Commission. His grandfather, in his long years as a radio evangelist and founder of this seminary, had brought multitudes to faith. Harold, as far as he knew, had never managed one solitary soul. He wondered why it didn't matter more to him.

The park occupied forty acres in the center of the city, adjacent to the city zoo where peacocks ranged free and often burst awkwardly over the fences to sashay among the park's occupants, looking for handouts. Harold liked the extravagant birds and tossed them bread crusts and apple slices. A large, murky pond speckled with ducks wrapped the south edge of the park, with walking paths winding in and out of trees, and exercise stations at intervals. Harold would wander the paths, sometimes for an hour or more before returning to classes. He found he could walk and read at the same time—nearly the only way he could stay with *Abstract on Systematic Theology* without drifting into semiconsciousness. On his walks he often got the sense of someone following him. Yet when he glanced back, no one was ever there but the peacocks.

He sat at the same bench every day, carefully opening his sack lunch beside him—an egg salad sandwich, a dill pickle, a sliced Honeycrisp apple, and a bottle of blue Gatorade. Almost daily, he saw an attractive woman sitting at a bench nearby, eating lunch from a ziploc she kept in a black carryall bag. She wore the loose blue scrubs of a nurse or medical technician. She rarely looked his way, and her aloofness bothered him. Once, when he tossed his partially eaten apple slice to a peacock, he saw her watching. He smiled at her, but she didn't return it, and her indifference deflated him for hours.

Harold was twenty-seven, had known several friendly relationships with women but nothing serious. He was a tad overweight but, in his estimation, not bad looking. Yet lately he'd begun to feel life passing him by; he fretted about it at night. Making a decision to seek a spiritual path seemed reasonable, even wise at this point in time. He didn't drink or smoke. Though sex often occupied his thoughts, his experience was minimal. He couldn't list many sins beyond those of omission. The life he'd led had been watchful, rarely reckless (though at college he'd once stolen a yield sign for his dorm room). Lacking the material for a dramatic testimony, he possessed in its place an impressively spotless character, which seemed worth something in this environment. He felt no strong sense of call to a spiritual life yet assumed, given his heritage, that it would come in time.

His mother lurked in the background, applauding his decision. She was ardently religious and had raised him as she was raised. Harold's father, an easy-going, unambitious man, had left years before, battered by her stiff disapproval. The last Harold had heard from him, he was tending bar in Santa Monica.

Several months ago, in early summer, Harold had moved back home with her—the house only a twenty-minute drive from school.

She'd offered to pay his tuition since she had long dreamed of him carrying on family tradition (her father was the radio evangelist). He didn't refuse her in spite of uneasiness about her expectations.

So Harold left a career as a sound technician for a community college on the east side of the state—a job that engaged him but required long hours, many dull assignments, and mediocre pay. He'd imagined becoming sound mixer for some musical group doing concerts around the world, but those jobs never seemed to materialize. As a boy he'd imagined even more. He'd once fancied himself…what was it…a spaceflight commander?

Harold needed new challenges, more meaningful commitments. A life of serving God seemed a logical choice.

His first chance to do just that came sooner than he expected. On a Friday as he ate his egg salad sandwich in the park, he noticed the same attractive woman at her bench having lunch. But today she was crying, wiping her eyes with a large handkerchief. He sat rigidly, not knowing what to do. Finally, he forced himself to his feet and went to her.

"Are you all right?" he asked uncertainly.

She shook her head, seeming irritated at his intrusion.

On an impulse, he asked, "May I pray for you?"

With a sigh, she moved over and made room.

He sat down beside her and bowed his head. He wanted to lay a hand on her shoulder but didn't dare. "Lord, this lamb of your flock is in pain and in need of your help. Come to her and give her comfort, give her loving support in her time of difficulty. Whatever is making her suffer, take it away, Lord. Let her know she belongs to you. Let her know she is valued and loved. And…umm…" As always (lacking his grandfather's facility), he could get a prayer airborne but had trouble landing it. "Amen," he trailed off. He cleared his throat.

"Thanks," she said impassively.

He offered his hand, but she didn't take it. "My name is Harold."

"A New Vision student, right? I'm afraid you've misread the situation, Harold. I'm not crying. I have a bug in my eye. The thing feels big as a cockroach. Maybe you could get it out." She pulled down a lower lid, and he leaned close, inhaling the faint aroma of lavender. Her eyes were lined in purple and hooded in blackish green. Even in scrubs, her body seemed a pleasing combination of delicate and plush, a down pillow.

"I see it in the far corner. May I use your handkerchief?" It took him only a moment to wipe out the bug. He flicked it from her cheek with a finger.

"You're an answer to prayer," she said dryly, blinking multiple times. "Lousy bug." She took her handkerchief back, wiped her eye and blew her nose. "At least you didn't ask me if Jesus Christ was my Lord and Savior."

He smiled and shrugged.

"Is there some contest for souls going on at school? New Vision students have nearly chased me out of the park. I try not to make eye contact."

"I know, I know."

"You do?" She seemed surprised.

"It's presumptuous. It doesn't work."

She sat not speaking for several moments. "Hmm…you're a curious one." She put a carrot in her mouth and crunched it. "I see you feeding peacocks. Do you like them?"

"I do. They're interesting creatures."

She smiled at him for the first time. "I appreciate your thoughtfulness, Harold, even if I didn't need the prayer. I'm Avis."

He shook her outstretched hand, warm as a bun, then stood and returned to his bench with an even warmer pulsing in his temples. She had an edge, wore too much makeup for his taste, but he found her presence…well, electrifying.

It only took a short time before the seminary staff learned about Harold's previous life as a sound technician. They suddenly had need of him everywhere, especially in chapel services. Because the skill seemed to raise his stock with faculty, he agreed to most of the jobs, though the pay could not even be called modest. Part of the deal was training volunteer assistants, the first a soft, plump Dutch girl named Hilda—naïve and sheltered, but aglow with health, twenty-two, and clearly interested in him. He didn't return the feeling, but she refused to notice. Hilda quickly learned the basics of the digital mixer, softening his feelings toward her. Yet when he dreamed, he dreamed of Avis, the girl in the park.

Avis didn't show up at lunchtime for a week or more after the eye incident, but then one day she reappeared. He was taking a drink of blue Gatorade when he saw her sit down on her bench and wave to him. He gathered up his lunch and went over.

"Hi." He led with his warmest smile.

"Hello, Harold," she replied nonchalantly.

"I haven't seen you lately."

"I've been busy." She opened a plastic bag of trail mix. He sat beside her.

"Just out of curiosity, are you a nurse?"

"I was until a while ago. I still wear my scrubs to work. Nursing was good. I liked helping people. But I needed a more creative life."

"Like what?"

"Body art...I'm a tattoo artist, newly licensed."

Harold swallowed hard. He hid his shock but felt a bit sick.

She laughed. "I can see the demons dancing in your head."

She was accurate about that. "Do you work at Eye of the Peacock?"

"It's the only one around. We don't have the best reputation among New Vision folk. Still, we've become quite respectable these days."

"But...you aren't even tattooed."

"I am, but not where you can see."

Harold had a fleeting erotic thought about one day being invited for a viewing. Just then, a peacock meandered by so close that a tail feather brushed his pant leg.

"Oh my God, a peacock just touched you. They're spiritual birds, Harold. It's a sign—a symbol of new beginnings…an awakening." The peacock wandered away, oblivious.

He brightened, explaining that he'd just left his last job, moved back home with his mother to attend the seminary his grandfather had founded. "It *is* a new beginning—of a more spiritual life."

Her response was less enthusiastic than he hoped. "Hmmm. You moved back with your mother to attend your grandfather's seminary? Sounds like climbing back in the womb to me. Was it your idea or your mother's?"

He reddened. "Mine…mostly."

"Well, there are other ways of being spiritual, you know." She took a deep breath. "Does anyone call you Harry?"

"No. It's always been Harold."

She crunched on the trail mix and drank from a water bottle. "What job did you leave?"

"Sound technician at a college."

Her face lit up. "That's interesting. I could use somebody like you."

Harold grew wary. "For what?"

"My band."

"You have a band, too?"

"I'm lead singer and keyboardist."

Uneasy now, imagining more pro bono work, he changed the subject. "Would you like half an egg salad sandwich? Your lunch looks like rabbit food."

She laughed. "Sure, thanks." She reached for his half sandwich, sniffed it, and took a bite. "This is good. Did your mother make it?"

He nodded. "Egg salad every day. It's my favorite."

"Every day—goodness. Such consistency."

He glanced at her. Was she making fun of him? "I guess I'm like that."

"We are what we are, Harry." She had another bite of egg salad. He offered her a pickle, and she took it. "Could you drop by my place some night? I just bought a used sound mixer. It's ancient and there's no manual for it. The machine is a mystery to me, Harry. I live above Eye of the Peacock. Stairway is in the back."

"Your place?"

"How about Tuesday?"

Harold shocked himself by saying yes. She seemed intent on calling him Harry. He didn't really mind.

For Friday's chapel service, Hilda did her first solo run on sound with Harold observing. Afterwards, alone together in the sound room as they put away equipment, he was lavish with his praise, hoping to flatter her into taking over the dull task. His positive words seemed to switch on a light in her. Her skin glowed a soft, kewpie doll pink.

"I never knew sound could be this fun. You're a wonderful teacher, Harold."

"Well, it's easy with such a capable student."

She removed the batteries from a handheld microphone and put them in a charger. Her hands trembled as she did it. "I have a secret I'd like to share with you, but you can't tell anybody. Not a living soul. Do you promise?"

"Well…sure."

"Could we go into the recording booth?"

The small room was padded, windowless, with a lock on the door. He was curious and nervous as he followed her in. "Really? Is it that much of a secret?"

"I think it is." She locked the door behind them. "I want to know we're safe. I have to lift my sweater up to show you."

Something frog-like leaped in Harold's stomach. Hilda raised her yellow cashmere sweater up over her white bra. Her breasts were full, and the bra was sturdy and straining.

"I really like you, Harold, or I wouldn't be doing this. It's very personal. I have to unhook my bra to show you."

Harold took a deep breath. "Okay."

She reached back and deftly opened three separate clasps. With hand and forearm, she held both cups in place. "Under the strap near my arm. See it?"

He moved closer and did see it—a small, purple tattoo of a peacock.

Her voice was low, intimate. "If the school found out, I don't know what would happen. It's just a tiny tattoo but very meaningful to me. I've only shown one girlfriend and now you—I trust you both."

"It's nice," he said, meaning more than just the tattoo.

"You can touch it if you'd like."

Harold hesitated, and then brushed his fingertips over the spot. "You have beautiful skin." He wasn't lying. Her skin was milky white, softer even than her cashmere sweater.

"I take care of it." She didn't seem to mind that he kept his fingers on her skin. "You have such a gentle touch."

Harold's brain and body were running riot. He was desperate to slide his fingers into her loose bra cup but his hand seemed to be frozen in place. He felt very dizzy. He shook his head and cleared his throat. "Uhh, who did the tattoo, Hilda?" His voice was more of a squawk.

She seemed to be having her own hormonal struggles, but the question released a bit of the tension. "This girl at Eye of the Peacock. I was thinking of a dove, but she talked me into a tiny peacock. She was an apprentice then, so it was free. I tipped her of course."

"Was her name Avis?"

Startled, Hilda said, "Yes, do you know her?"

"A little. But never mind her. You really are attractive. I feel very drawn to you, Hilda."

She nodded, obviously understanding what he meant. With sudden resolve, she reached back and fastened her bra. Her shallow, rapid breathing matched his own. "Goodness, I didn't realize how stimulating this would be. I apologize. I didn't mean to tempt you."

"Maybe I could see your tattoo again some time."

She pulled her sweater into place. "If we get more serious, you will see it again, Harold." She smiled and blushed. "That's a promise." She leaned into him and kissed his cheek.

On Sunday, his mother asked him to accompany her to morning worship at her church, and as usual he begged off because he attended services every weekday at school. Their living situation was still new enough that she was careful with him, restraining her usual commanding nature, relaxing her menacing brow. He'd been away enough years that he almost believed she'd mellowed. She wore a lacy green eyelet dress and her bird's nest hat, carried her black leather Bible in one hand, white lace gloves in the other. She was still in her mid-fifties, young enough to crave another try at matrimony, but the church's population was dwindling and most available males were aging widowers.

She had hopes for Harold, too. "The seminary is a wonderful place to meet like-minded partners. Have you met any nice girls, dear?"

The question annoyed him. He knew the school had a secondary function as evangelical matchmaking service. "They're mostly young and immature, mother."

"I don't see why that should matter."

"Well, there is one possibility. I'm training her on the sound mixer. We seem to be making some progress."

His mother's face brightened. "Oh, how lovely. What's her name?"

"Hilda."

"You must bring Hilda home for dinner some evening."

"Let's give it a little time, mother. If things develop, then maybe so."

"Of course, son." She floated out the door looking pleased.

He thought about Hilda's hidden tattoo and wondered if inviting her to dinner might inspire a fuller unveiling.

Harold had rarely doubted that he was among the chosen, yet the orbit of his recent fantasies troubled him. Since entering the seminary, he seemed to have more and more to pray about. Yet he also reminded himself that there was more joy in heaven over one repentant sinner than over the faultless ninety-nine with no need for it.

Harold was nervous and inattentive in his Tuesday classes. He ate his lunch in the cafeteria and bought his dinner there, too, letting his mother know he'd be working late in the library. Not wishing his car to be seen near the tattoo parlor, he decided to walk. It was late September, and the sun was already low in the sky. As he passed the zoo entrance, he once again felt he was being followed. Seconds later he heard a low growling just behind—he stopped and froze in place. After a moment, he nervously turned. A large peacock stood facing him, its green tail feathers spread and purple neck puffed. Its sounds were angry, the beak and talons lethal-looking, the beady black eyes menacing. Alarmed, Harold tried hard to calm himself; he slowly turned away, moved several tentative steps, bracing for an attack from behind. When it didn't come and he'd travelled a fair distance, he dared to look back. The bird had resumed normal size and was pecking about for insects.

Still, he was shaken. Was it some sort of message related to his present motives? Harold took a long, slow breath, calming his heart, forcing himself to think rationally. No doubt he'd come too close to a peahen's nesting site (wasn't it late in the year for nesting, though?). On the return trip he would simply give the area a wide berth.

Eye of the Peacock occupied the ground floor of an old Victorian house painted cranberry red. The sign featured a large peacock with tail feathers spread, the feathered eyes painted to resemble human ones. Harold looked the place over, saw a light on the second floor, and walked a narrow driveway to the back. There he found an old Dodge van and next to it a wooden staircase leading to a second-floor porch. He smoothed his hair, checked his fly, and went up, the steps creaking ominously. Avis was standing at the door when he arrived. She was not in her scrubs but wore dark green tights and a snug, sleeveless purple tee shirt. For the first time he got a clear sense of her remarkable body.

"Right on time, Harry," she said. "Come on in."

The apartment was a shock, hung with drawings of what looked like tattoo designs, among them many peacocks. Behind the drawings, walls were a tomato soup color, the ceiling black. An upright piano, a keyboard, and speakers filled one corner. The few pieces of furniture scattered about looked like vintage Goodwill. Another young woman, feral-looking with spiky orange hair, surprised him. She was pouring red wine in the kitchen. She wore shorts and a tank top, and, except for her face, she was covered in tattoos. The heavy sweetness of incense hung in the room, chunks of amethyst crystals and geodes cluttered end tables, and candles burned in a dozen places. Harold felt as if he'd stepped into some pagan underworld.

"Rita," Avis said, "Meet Harry, the sound guy. I don't know his last name."

"Flowers," Harold said.

"Harry Flowers, this is Rita Gomez, my lead guitarist."

"How are ya?" Rita asked. "Want some wine?"

"No thanks."

"Weed?"

Avis laughed. "He's a New Vision student."

"Well, too bad. So what's wrong with some wine, Harry? Jesus drank it all the time."

Harold made an effort to smile. "Maybe later."

Rita shrugged. "Whatever…more for us."

"Harry likes peacocks. That's kind of how we met." Avis led Harold to a lumpy gold chair.

"Well, that's a plus," Rita said. "I like 'em, too." She pointed to a small peacock on her upper arm and a larger one on her thigh.

"Did you do those?" Harold asked Avis.

"No, it was my boss, Iron John. He's a senior artist, a master. I'm just an intermediate."

"I'm one of his masterpieces," Rita announced and swallowed some wine. "Some people, especially guys, stare at me like I'm hanging in the Louvre. Sometimes it's a bother, but there are worse problems to have, right, Avis?"

"To each his own," Avis replied with her usual nonchalance. "The sound mixer is on the piano, Harry. You want to see it?"

Instead of sitting, he followed her. The mixer was an old Avid analog. He needed only a glance to know it was probably a good buy. "It should work for a small band," he said.

"There're only four of us, Harry. Could you come to a gig and try it out? Just show me how to do it one time, and I'll take it from there."

He hesitated, and then his tongue moved contrary to his will. Her presence melted all objections. "I guess I could do that."

She smiled broadly, leaned and kissed him on the ear. His heart flipped like a hooked fish. "You're very sweet, Harry. I owe you for this. Friday night at the Walleye Bar out on the road to the beach. First two drinks are free to the band—and of course to my soundman. If you want, you can come here first and ride with me...seven okay?"

"I guess I could do that," he said, a quaver in his voice.

Having dreamed of piloting a ship at flank speed toward a massive iceberg, he staggered from bed the next morning with heart pounding. He made a point to catch Hilda at the sound board during chapel. He asked her to dinner at his mother's on Thursday. Hilda was stunned; she actually got misty-eyed. Harold found this embarrassing, yet felt a certain comfort in her soft, sentimental nature, knowing that just across the park dwelt a siren luring him to the rocks.

Thanks to Harold's mother, he was able to learn a number of basic biographical facts as they ate her chicken divan, famous at church potlucks. Hilda's father was an Iowa farmer with a large dairy herd. Hilda was the fourth of six children. Her mother was organist at their church. Hilda listened to Christian radio most of the time (did she say that just to impress his mother?). Only by thinking about her tiny tattoo could Harold keep from dozing off. He suspected there had to be more to her, something rebellious and passionate. His great problem, however, was having nowhere to take her to find out. He lived in his mother's house. Hilda lived in a dorm where no males were allowed. His car was small and cramped—but, unless they took to the woods, it would have to do.

Toward the end of their blessedly brief evening, while Hilda was in the bathroom, Harold's mother delivered her assessment: "She's a lovely girl, Harold. Very good values. She didn't take out her cell phone even once. She doesn't match you in intellect, but she has nice skin. And her family, I suspect, is well off. I imagine after a few children, she will grow beyond her present attractive plumpness. She looks the type. Not many of us can stay fit after child bearing. All in all, though, you certainly could do worse."

This, for her, was affirmation. "I plan to take it slowly, mother."

She laughed quietly. "Oh, I know, Harold. Slow is your middle name. But you'll be thirty before long. You might try shifting into second gear, if you get what I mean."

Harold blushed at the implication.

As he drove Hilda back toward the seminary, he put on some quiet jazz. "Do you really listen to Christian radio all the time, Hilda?"

"Well, I like the music, but I like this, too."

"That's…good to know."

"I can't wait for you to meet my parents. Your mother is sweet."

"You think so? I guess she has her moments." He felt a touch of indigestion from the chicken divan. "It's still early. Want to go out to the beach and watch the waves?"

"That sounds really nice. Just remember my ten o'clock curfew."

"An unreasonable time, don't you think?"

"Well, it's eleven on the weekends."

They parked on a bluff overlooking Lake Michigan. The sun was gone, but the sky glowed the color of Hilda's cheeks. Only two other cars, widely spaced, occupied the lot.

"Isn't this place called Make Out Point?" she asked.

"Maybe. I'm not sure. It's a nice place to view the scenery."

"Not many cars here, thankfully."

"Yeah. I'm glad."

She quietly cleared her throat and touched his hand resting on the shift lever. "Could we talk a minute about personal boundaries, Harold?"

Indigestion began to burn in the area of his sternum. "You can trust me, Hilda."

"Oh, I know that. I just wanted to say that petting is totally fine with me, but I'd like to save intercourse for marriage."

Her businesslike manner dazed him, yet he gathered himself. "Umm, just what do you mean by petting, Hilda? I'm not entirely familiar with the term."

"Oh, you know—kissing and fondling each other."

"But without intercourse."

"That's right."

He nodded, still disbelieving. "You mean I can see your tattoo again?"

Soft and serene as a lap cat, she curled against him.

The following night, tight with apprehension, Harold left his car at school and walked around the park to avoid peacocks. Hilda's petting had left him feeling crazed; vestiges of it remained: his legs were heavy, his head light as a helium balloon. The thought of Avis in tights and tee shirt didn't help. When he reached Eye of the Peacock, he paused to look more closely at the large painted peacock with dozens of human eyes on its tail. They seemed to move with him as he passed.

It was seven p.m. and still light. Avis, now in shorts and a man's shirt, was loading her keyboard into the van. Harold rushed to help. He carried down two pole mount speakers and then the sound mixer. She had a suitcase full of charts and a large tip jar.

"So much crap to haul around. It's work, Harry, and the pay sucks. I do all the booking…I pay the band and split up the tips. Good thing it's fun once we start or I'd quit in a minute." At that, she rushed inside and returned quickly in a short black dress covered in spangles. She carried a hairbrush and zippered makeup bag. "Drive, Harry, would you? I gotta put on my face."

"Your face doesn't need it."

She flashed a smile; he felt the buzz and tingling of nervous anticipation. He'd dressed up in a sport coat and khakis, his chapel outfit, and hoped he looked the part of a band guy.

"The brakes pull to the right," she said and climbed in the passenger side, tossing two fast food bags into the back seat. She turned down the visor and used the mirror to do her eyes.

As he navigated the narrow driveway, he asked, "Your sign out front—why human eyes on the peacock's tail?"

"Iron John did that. They're not exactly human. They're supposed to be the hundred eyes of God."

"What are the hundred eyes of God?"

She glanced at him with a touch of impatience. "You probably don't get into much Greek mythology at New Vision. See, the giant Argos had a hundred eyes. When he was killed, Zeus's wife put his eyes on the peacock's tail to make him immortal. If you're into Christianity those peacock eyes mean immortality, too—not to mention God, who sees every move you make." She took out a lipstick and swiped it on in with amazing precision. It was the color of her apartment walls. Harold, chilled by her explanation, stared a moment at those gleaming lips and then rallied—recklessly considering a drink or two that evening.

The Walleye Bar served food to a crowd that doubled in size once the band began. Hiding his unease, Harold set up the sound mixer and balanced levels for each instrument. Avis was ecstatic. "You're amazing, Harry!" she exclaimed, locking him in a hug. Avis introduced him to her bass man, a weirdly thin guy named Sid, wrapped in tight leather with legs like black soda straws, and her drummer Clyde, burly as a lumberjack who came straight from a construction site in a tee shirt and jeans, his work boots sprinkled with sawdust. Rita wore a short, sexy dress that flaunted her tattoos. Avis called her band The Tattoos, since body art was visible on all but her. The crowd already knew that her body art was hidden in some private place, and each night (Rita told him) the drunks would beg for a peek. It was a come-on that worked week after week.

To Harold's surprise, The Tattoos were good, but Avis stole the show. She billed them as a cover band, and their music was all over the map—no special choreographed dance steps—they simply played and enjoyed it. She could sing jazz with a quiet bass accompaniment, belt out a country ballad, and kill her own version of "Rag Doll." He was mesmerized. He sat at the end of bar near the sound board; the bartender set a beer in front of him. Harold nodded his thanks and took a sip. It was dark and bitter, not very pleasant, but fairly soon he had another. The bartender was a huge, intimidating man with shaved head and jagged scar crossing his skull on a diagonal. When he caught Harold staring at it, he said, "Brain transplant, man."

At the end of the first set, she introduced each band member, then her new soundman Harry Flowers (his heart lifted at the applause), and finally herself. Her full name was Avis Swift. The crowd was loud, drunk, and danced like fools—as if they actually thought they could.

Harold initially found them obnoxious but began to feel more amicable as the night wore on.

It was two in the morning before Avis paid the band and packed up. Harold loaded her equipment into the van, feeling a small but noteworthy part of the entertainment scene.

"Are you okay to drive?" Avis asked, climbing into the passenger seat.

"I had two beers. Maybe three. I'm fine." In truth, he was buzzed, flying on alcohol and adrenalin. He grinned hazily.

"Yeah, but you don't drink."

"Maybe I'm changing."

"Oh, nice. I'm already corrupting you."

"I wouldn't mind going along to the next gig, Avis. I didn't get much chance to show you the mixer."

She looked askance at him. "Okay with me…you do make a difference."

"Your voice is amazing with or without it."

She smiled at that. "You're pretty nice to me, Harry."

"You keep surprising me," he said. At that, they went quiet. The van rolled into town and soon swung into Eye of the Peacock. "I'll help you in with the stuff."

"It's late, Harry. You have to drive home yet. I'll do it."

He helped her anyway. When they were done, she flopped into a chair and asked if he'd like a glass of wine. She needed one, and she promised to drive him to his car afterwards. Harold was in no mood to refuse her anything. With each sip of Chardonnay, he felt his edges dulling. She dozed off with a wine glass in her hand. Harold caught it before it tipped and set it on a table beside her. He stood over her, drifting slightly to the right, staring dreamily down. Her eyes opened just a crack.

"What, Harry? Oh…you probably want to see my tattoo." She yawned heavily.

He hesitated, surprised. "I'd love to, Avis."

She stood and in one motion pulled her black dress over her head. Her underwear was black and miniscule. Her tattoo was a single peacock feather with a heart-shaped eye near her breast and curving down to her hip. The spines of the feather were black, the feather green, the eye a small black heart surrounded by a blue heart, surrounded by another the color of her lipstick.

"It's very…I'd have to say…understated. It's lovely. Did Long John do it?"

She snorted. "*Iron* John. Hardly. He's not into understatement. I did it myself using mirrors. It took a month."

Harold drifted the other way, his head full of whipped cream. "Amazing. May I touch it?"

"I guess…if you need to."

He ran his fingers from top to bottom and back. "Your skin is soft as moonlight."

"God, Harry, that's poetic. You must be drunk. You don't seem like the same guy."

"I am the same guy."

"You better stay here tonight. If a cop stops you, your religious career won't be worth jack squat."

Harold texted his mother to tell her he was staying the night with a friend. It wasn't a lie. His thumbs weren't working, so Avis helped him send the message. She didn't have a couch. The only bed was hers. She seemed to have no qualms about sharing it.

Harold woke in a sunny room with a desert-dry mouth and a vague headache. Avis was already up and getting dressed in her scrubs. His own clothes were strewn about the floor near his side of the bed. He leaned up on an elbow to watch. He discovered he had nothing on.

"Where are you going?" he asked.

"I have a client this morning."

"Come back to bed."

"No time for it, Harry."

He sighed heavily. "I'm in love with you, Avis."

She laughed. "You're in love with the sex."

"I am, I admit it, but I'm really in love with you."

"Tell me something, Harry. Be honest. Was I your first?"

He pulled the sheet up to his chest. "That's very personal, Avis."

"I think I was."

His face began to burn. "Why would you ask?"

"Don't take offense. You were very nice. You have a few things to learn is all."

"What?"

"Just things."

"Show me. I'll do anything you want."

She sat on the gold chair to pull on her tennis shoes. "It's tempting, Harry, but I can't be late." She stood and moved toward the door. "Lock up when you leave. Just turn the thing on the knob."

"Wait, Avis. I know this seems way too fast, but I mean it. I really love you." More words poured out, and he had no idea where they were coming from. "If you should ever feel the same, I want to marry you."

She laughed and tossed him a kiss. "Go home, Harry. You don't want to marry me. You hardly know me. Anyway, I could never marry a preacher."

"How about a soundman?"

"You're a nice guy, but now you're getting weird. I think you're just discovering yourself—a little later than most. I think you're confused." She turned and hustled downstairs.

Feeling bereft and a bit sick to his stomach, Harold walked through the park toward the zoo. His emotions were tangled. Why had he asked her to marry him? He hadn't exactly meant to say it; he just didn't want to lose her. She was his opposite in every way, yet he was bewitched. He was sure his feelings were deeper and finer than just the sex. She had color and life; he was all grays and beiges. She was alive and glowing; he was a bland nonentity. He believed God would approve of his uncommon love for her. There had to be some special dispensation for the magic he felt. Did she feel it, too? In time, he knew she would. He hoped she would. She might. Maybe she wouldn't.

The zoo entrance was nearby. It was Saturday, and people with children would be lining up in an hour from now. Just as he realized he was in the place he'd vowed to avoid, something stabbed him in the hip. The pain was excruciating; he staggered sideways. He saw the big wings flapping just as needle-like talons clamped to his right shoulder and arm. The beak hit his temple like a hammer. Dazed, Harold clutched the purple neck and wrestled the bird to the ground, its wings flailing wildly. Talons released as the peacock struggled to find a footing. Harold held the beak as far from him as he could. "What the hell are you?" he cried. "What are you doing?" He gave the bird a hard shove and ran, leaving it dazed and reeling. He went straight to the college infirmary. His shoulder needed five stitches; his temple and hip were patched with butterfly bandages. His ripped and bloodied clothing went into a plastic bag for cleaning and repair. He made his way home in scrubs.

His mother brought him tea while he recuperated the remainder of Saturday and all of Sunday. He had a paper due on Dawson Burns, the great preacher and temperance campaigner, but felt no motivation to work. Hilda came by to console him, pray for him, and she talked so eagerly about a *Left Behind* book that she seemed to suck the oxygen out of the room. He asked her to call him Harry, and, though puzzled, she agreed. She finally left, kissing his cheek, and he rested a while, depressed.

He sat in his mother's recliner. A painting of his grandfather, the evangelist, hung on the wall above the fireplace. The great man always had the words (he claimed the Spirit provided them) for every occasion. He possessed in his memory an encyclopedic stock of prayers and platitudes. In any situation, he could call forth a prayer, a sermon line, a relevant Biblical passage, not even needing to think. He spoke with ease and authority, forever in control. It was a gift Harry had hoped one day to receive. As a boy, he was convinced the evangelist echoed the voice of God.

Oddly, the content of his grandfather's words was never what stuck—it was his style that impressed the boy. The mellifluous voice had, in truth, served as background music for young Harold's dreams of a brilliant life—dreams now long forgotten, like beloved stuffed animals in an attic. Yet yesterday something had shaken him like a dust mop, wounded him, but he'd stood and had it out, toe to toe.

Harry closed his eyes. He felt humbled. He felt alone. He sensed a distant, as yet indefinable blessing. And he began to remember.

www.ingramcontent.com/pod-product-compliance
Lightning Source LLC
Chambersburg PA
CBHW072128300726
48975CB00003B/970